NEW LEGENDS
THE HERO · THE ANTI-HERO · THE VIGILANTE

An Anthology

Within the world of 'Service' and the city of 'Goodness', there lies the neighborhood of, 'Intention' populated by individuals called, 'Techniques'. While the Techniques may dwell in the same locations and strive to share the same intentions for the greater good in order to serve the community and mankind alike . . .

. . . their actions are NOT the same. They are as different as the time of day and yet necessary for each day to exist and come to past.

NEW LEGENDS
THE HERO · THE ANTI-HERO · THE VIGILANTE

An Anthology

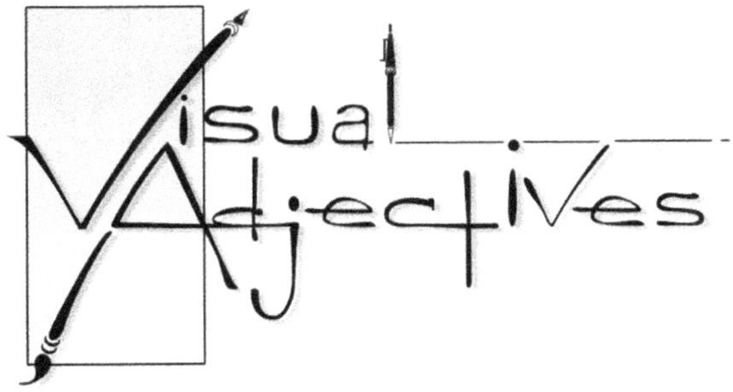

NEW LEGENDS
THE HERO • THE ANTI-HERO • THE VIGILANTE

Cover, pencil and ink by Edward J. Stinson Jr.
Cover design by Annabella Rios
Colors by Michelle Lawrence, John Mondelli

Published by Visual Adjectives, LLC, Delray Beach, Florida.

Visual Adjectives
14280 Military Trail, # 7501
Delray Beach, Florida 33482

Web: www.VisualAdjectives.com
E-mail: info@VisAdj.com

Library of Congress Control Number: 2013921101

ISBN-13: 978-0-9833329-2-3 (trade paperback)
ISBN-10: 0-9833329-2-4 (trade paperback)

First American Paperback Edition: November 2013

COPYRIGHT ACKNOWLEDGEMENTS

GENERAL LIBERTY

WEAPONXMITH
WEAPONXMITH

DARK AMERICA

INTRODUCTION

THE HERO · THE ANTI-HERO · THE VIGILANTE
By Edward J. Stinson Jr.

Heroes are the bright morning that we look forward to, the sunlight on our face, the promise of something better to come, and the clarity from the dreams and nightmares from the night of last. Heroes are the brunch, midday snack, and good news for the day. They're the smiles in the park and the waves to your neighbor. They're the flag streaming from the front porch and the hug of a loved one.

Antiheroes make up the sunset and the sunrise. They are the 'gray zone' between the day that leaves and the night that comes. They're the night passing into the new day promised. They're the ones that a person can point their finger at and say, there goes a hero', with as much vigor as another that is pointing their finger shouting, 'there goes a criminal!'

They're the early supper before your late-night show, your conversation about the late bills, and your heart-to-heart talk that you've been fretting to have with your loved one all day. They're your alarm ringing the next morning, your first sip of coffee, your traffic report, and your dreary ride to work. They connect the day to the night as well as the night to the day.

Vigilantes are the exhale of night which is as critical as the hero being the inhale of day. They are not conversation, question, or verbal response... they exists only as the action that must be taken.

They're vampires feeding off of the evil that they battle while cursing that same wickedness coursing through their veins. This is what makes them such a deadly tool. To understand a vigilante is to argue with another about their religion.

It does not work; for vigilantes are driven by the forces that have made them.

The night engulfed them ages ago and refused to allow them freedom from its clutch. Their road is lonely, allowing them to stop for quick breaks when the sunrise comes and the day has its chance on the playground. Vigilantes see themselves as the sand on the playground that MUST be there; for they cushion the blow when society falters.

The **Hero** focuses on stopping crime first and addressing evil second while following the law.

He strives to inspire, to be accountable to those he serve, and embraces the responsibility that comes with his position.

The **Antihero** focuses on stopping crime and stopping evil alike. He is willing to bend the law to accomplish his task.

He creates apprehension and inspires those that he has served and saved directly. He lacks accountability but embraces the responsibility of his position.

The **Vigilante** focuses on stopping evil first and addressing crime second and is willing to break the law.

He is terror. He exists as the necessary evil existing to rival the evil that he combats. He is not and cares not about accountability or responsibility. This is a path that he has no choice but to travel. He is the warring angel in the bowels of hell.

CONTENTS

SYNOPSIS

KNIGHT-HOOD AND CHIVALRY
By Edward J. Stinson Jr.
   A tale from the *THE ADVENTURES OF KNIGHT-HOOD*

A Real Life Super Hero finds himself battling for his very survival and questions the futility of his efforts to help people. He is amazed to learn how he is really seen by those he sought to help.

THE WHISPER AND FIORELLO
By Brady Dale

The Whisper is a unique superhero. His supernatural senses allow him to hear criminals in the act of planning crimes. He keeps track of them so well, that he seldom has to intervene directly. Instead, he directs the Philadelphia police to apprehend criminals in the act. In fact, he has done so well that super-crime is unheard of in Philadelphia, until one day a group attacks its Federal reserve. Except, the plan was never going to work... why did they even try?

That's the question on The Whisper's mind each night after doing his bit of crime fighting. That is, until he relaxes into the one sort of socializing he allows himself: completely anonymous online conversation. Except, is it really anonymous? Who is he talking to after all? And why is she always, always available?

A LESSON
By L. Andrea Mosier

In the aftermath of a school shooting, Quintessa Verge, the Memphis high school teacher who confronted a teenage gunman in her classroom, returns to her hometown to help journalist Jorge Rodriguez take politically charged photos of meth makers in rural Tennessee. But when the road takes a major detour, Tess learns that there are scarier things than a teenage gunman.

SYNOPSIS

DARK AMERICA
By Edward J. Stinson Jr.

The summations of two self-proclaimed heroes merge into a single event that spotlights the shrouded actions within America's forgotten soul... the common community.

FOR THE HONOR OF STROMGARD
By Suzannie M. Lawrence
A tale from the *ENDAERIA CHRONICLES*

Drinking away their latest spoils and trading tales, a group of cutthroats pick a fight with locals and gets more than they bargained for.

ANGELS AMONG US
By David Miller

Malakh
A minister starts his journey as a superhero: first with personal ministry to the homeless at night, then by attempting to stop a gang from attacking a homeless family.

Mitsukai
A young woman loses her parents in a car-bombing, meant for someone else. By day, she's a doctor at a local E.R. By night, she stalks the streets as a crime-fighting antihero, calling herself Mitsukai.

Nephilim
An orphan with a troubled past joins the Omi gang. He leaves when their crimes push him too far. He dedicates his life to raining down vengeance on all criminals. Maybe, one day, he will be redeemed.

Youkai
Continued from Nephilim. From a detective's point of view. In the

process of investigating a triple homicide, a detective stumbles upon a conspiracy that may spell doom.

POWER OF CHARISMA
By Edward J. Stinson Jr.
A tale from the *ELITE FORCES DIVISION*

Cal has a smile that can't be ignored... and 'extrabilities' to match. He is a troubled youth in turmoil as he becomes a pawn to his own rage, jealousy, and loss of control. With his new powers he is nothing more than a boy trying to create fear... that is, until he learns what fear truly is. A Ghosthawk appears, as one tasked to bring order to the standoff that Cal has started with the police.

THE SHADOW HUNTER
By Quintin Baker

The people of Haven were promised prosperity, peace, and security. These promises are all relative though, especially in a city ruled by vampires. Corruption runs unchecked, as innocent blood is spilled in the back alleys. But a force lies in shadows of the city with the power to fight back. Amiris, a mysterious young man, with otherworldly powers, battles to bring light to a city spiraling into darkness.

WEAPONXMITH
By Adeleye Yussuf

William Carson was a doctor of science and a source of hope trapped in a world of corruption and crime. He was assigned to create the solution to his cities despair, this he did at the price of his life. He has designed guns to fell armies and armor to hold against the mightiest deathblows, but his greatest weapon was the one that he loved the most... his son.

Young Mark is something other than normal. He is the result of weapon technology integrated with the living human form. His limits are his creativity and his challenge is mercy. He strives to protect the innocent while struggling against the path of the damned; this is not the easiest path for the youth. Mark has become the ultimate weapon; now it is up to his humanity to become the WeaponXmith.

MILKMAN
By Edward J. Stinson Jr.

Evil is a concept that is intimate to all that experience it, as is goodness to all that apply it. There are those that need to be sacrificed in order for the blessings of righteousness to be realized. This is the plight of an unknown youth with an innocent smile, noble intentions, and a second personality inhabited by his father's rage.

BULLY
By Quintin Baker

ASSets Strip Club is an ordinary, run of the mill, seedy hole in the wall. Its owner rules the city's underground with an iron fist of corruption, murder and greed. Enter Bully, another beautiful and sexy young girl whose life is seemingly fated to entertain the darker desires of men. Instead, she hides her need for revenge against the man who wronged her and her family.

THE VEIL
By Edward J. Stinson Jr.
A tale from the *ENDAERIA CHRONICLES*

They are hatred formed as one, punishment gathered to be dispatched, nightmares born from pain, and nothing less than death to those they target. They are a soft spoken tale too dark to become legend and yet passed on by those who dare. The Veil is an organization whose members are the poisoned blade to be used by royalty and their god. They are demon reapers and tonight they have initiates.

NYTE'S TOY

By Suzannie M. Lawrence

A tale from the *ENDAERIA CHRONICLES*

Nyte, an assassin using whatever resources she can to accomplish her mission and protect her kingdom, is a Shade of the Shadow Communion. The elite assassin's guild, whose loyalty to the ruling family of Saenia has been unquestionable for the last 25 generations.

Something has been feeding on mortals and with the kingdom in political and social turmoil, it's her job to find out who or what. Her assignment leads her and her companion to a local inn, where she discovers her target.

ARCLIGHT

By Karl Joseph

What if you found yourself in a world of superheroes and villains? A world where anything from the comics took form and had substance? Now, imagine yourself in that world but with a different attitude and detesting those same heroes. That is the case of one teenage Glen Matterson, a self-proclaimed hipster who finds heroes and villains cliché and annoying. That all changes one day when Glen finds himself blessed (or was it cursed?) with the Meta gene gifting him extraordinary abilities. Will Glen implode in a ball of teenage self-loathing or step up to the path fate has laid out for him?

★ EDWARD J. STINSON JR. ★

KNIGHT-HOOD AND CHIVALRY

"My blood stinks," thinks the lonely masked figure pulling himself behind a deep alleyway dumpster next to a small brood of roaches.

He pulls the bottom of his mask up just above his nose before coughing with a rasp spitting a snot-full of crimson mucus. His body comes down slowly from his adrenalin high.

"I ain't a warrior..." he sputters in a conversation with himself, "I ain't a warrior." He repeats, as the feeling begins to leave his blood-covered legs sticking out from the side of a small trash pile collected next to the container. His sweat makes his mask itchy and his fear makes him anxious.

"G-gotta breathe... gotta keep breathing."

He leans against the damp brick wall and watches as the roaches scuttle over his waist getting caught on the thick gobs of his life fluid gathered in the gaps of his leather belt. His stomach wound is deep, as is the gash on the underside of his left arm. They burn with new felt pain now that the excitement is over. He dares to lean forward, but he has to check.

"Is he alive?!?" He hears in the distance.

He leans back once again trying to use his good arm to move the wet cardboard box beside him down towards his feet to hide them better. His breath gives out for a moment and panic screams as a best friend telling him to fight. The old-giving man pushes against the wall as tears begin to run from his eyes only to hide within the stitches of his mask. He wants to breathe so bad... and with a gasp, another breath comes.

"Puh-Please, God... I don't want to die!" He tries to shout while merely mustering a whisper.

The chill of death was close but the old man would not allow his warmth for life to leave.

"Yo, that bastard went this way, Tony!" Calls out a voice from the dim outer-alley lights. "Get Deuce to tha car, I'll take care of that fucker!"

"It's time," the old man resolves to himself.

There are only seconds left and he is so tired. He tried to wrap his arm earlier with one of his socks, but the knife wound left it as soaked as a sponge, freshly pulled from a sink filled with dirty dishwater.

The stab to his stomach spewed fluid and blood together, outlining a clear trail to his location. The stench is just awful enough to cover the urine smell of the wet concrete and alley trash.

"Fifteen years of feeding the homeless and I'm gonna die from saving a prostitute," he thinks to himself. "My first superhero fight..." He tries to laugh as he develops a light headache from blood loss.

Footsteps patter with sharp splashes at the edge of the alleyway as the masked man feels a new sensation from the blood running from his nose across his lips. It was salty. The dimness overtaking his sight reminds panic that this was a fight that it was destined to lose as be becomes weaker. His warmth fails as the chill moves beyond his skin and into his soul. The old masked man forgets to be afraid as darkness comes.

Light.
Beeps.
Phones ringing.
Morning.
"You okay, sir?" Asks a soft spoken voice, much like that imagined of an angel. "Can you see me? Here look at my fingers. How many do I have up?"

"Two," his tired voice responds. "Where..?"

"Shhh, don't worry, sir. You're going to be alright. You've been out for a while." The angelic nurse says while rubbing his wrist.

She smiles at the old man only to realize that she can't see his attempt to smile back. He raises his hand slowly to rub his face and discovers cloth and stitches protecting it.

"M – My mask?!?" He questions.

The nurse nods slowly with a new grin and shifts her eyes over to the guests sitting at the foot of his bed sleep. They are shoddy, dirty, weak, and homeless... but they are here for him.

She returns her focus to him. "They called the police for you. They've been here for the last two days and they made sure that we didn't remove your mask."

"What..?" He asks.

She completes her task of taking his pulse, checking his bandages, and raises the back of his bed to sit him up. The angel of a nurse swallows slowly while tucking his sheet into the side of his bed.

"You were a mess when you came in here, sir. They found your missing shoe." Her eyes glimmer as she stops what she is doing to stand before the old man.

"They said that you took care of them. It was difficult, but we worked around the mask issue and you should be okay. I don't know who you are or what you've done for these people, but they are calling you their savior."

The angel rubs his hand softly, "They are calling you... their superhero."

She then leaves the room allowing the old masked man time to cry alone.

★ BRADY DALE ★

THE WHISPER AND FIORELLO

Philadelphia was attacked by super villains for the first time in a decade and the best coverage came from WHYY - the public radio station. It went down right next door to their studios. When all the other reporters were shut out of the area, the microphone posse was already there. The anchor for the evening provided the coverage, rather than one of the assignment reporters, which was unusual. They also had photos and a supplemental firsthand account by a summer intern. Completely non-death-defying events in other parts of the city had all the regular journalists out of reach. Four white vans screeched to a halt outside the WHYY studios, blocking up the wide thoroughfare outside, causing a commotion that the anchor and the intern could hear from the newsroom. The vans didn't stop in front of the station, though. They stopped in front of its next door neighbor, the Federal Reserve Bank of Philadelphia.

Two or three hundred cars honked like preschoolers waiting for their snack as these four white vans caused an instant traffic jam all the way up into the Walt Whitman Bridge and back down into New Jersey. Aggravated commuters making it into work late that morning found themselves incomprehensibly frustrated. All of them honked, that is, all except those who could see what was going on up front. They stayed quiet. They wished no one would move at all.

Attuned to sounds, the veteran newshound perked up at the slightly changed timbre of the AM cacophony, and he dispatched his intern to go out front and find out if anything was going on. She went at the brisk pace of the focused young woman from the Upper Midwest that she was.

Once she was out of the newsroom, he heard the crashes.

Those would have been the sound of a Volvo and a Honda flying into the doors of the national bank and destroying the door's security measures. The anchor got up from his chair and grabbed a Marantz mini-disc reporter's recording rig and started moving for the door. He knew the sounds were no ordinary car crash.

"Coburn," he called out. "Snag your camera and come out front."

As soon as he got in the hall he found it full of people hot-footing it for the back. The late middle-age black woman that manned the front desk had her head down in a prayerful pose but she was shaking her head "no, no, no" as she made her way away from her post as quickly as possible.

He found the intern coming his way, fighting back tears as she crossed her arms in front of her chest and said, "Monsters!"

Monsters?

She must mean super-thugs, but how could that be? Super villains?

This was Philadelphia, the home of The Whisper. The estimable anchor knew for certain now that there was a story in front of their building. Super villains or something else and there was no one around to cover it but him so he was going out there.

"You coming?" He asked the intern.

She nodded and tears fell. Coburn, a small middle aged woman who looked like she'd rather be rock climbing, held up her camera and gave him a quick nod and went with him toward the melee. WHYY's building is big. So they were still a ways away when the three formed up, but they could hear the chaos growing.

It wouldn't last a lot longer, though.

As they came out front they saw The Most Amazing Man. People in New York City called him that. One of his many, many nicknames. The Most Amazing Man was more frequently referred to as "Fiorello," maybe the greatest hero in the entire world, the Defender of the Big Apple, the Charming Speedster.

They saw Fiorello come to a stop in front of the Federal Reserve Bank, about 100 yards south of their front entrance. According to the report they filed later, he stopped, grinned and gave the villains a sarcastic smile and an elaborate bow. Then he took the eight super thugs down like a French Savate Champion disarming angry spelling bee contestants attempting to waylay him with tennis rackets.

The anchor would spend almost a week deconstructing what he saw in the minute or so that he watched the attempted robbery fall apart. Anyone would be initially impressed or terrified - depending on your sensibility - by the eight threats that piled out of the four white vans. Exploder. Troll. Arch Stone. Pulverize. Ballistic and Raze. Force Field. And finally Hail-Falling-As-Doom-at-End-Times. The eight of them together could probably have faced down the combined armed forces of Canada and prevailed. All of them against a bank - even a Federal Bank - no problem.

All of them against Fiorello - no chance.

As if a super villain attack in Philadelphia were not big enough, Fiorello appearing made it all even bigger. When the first of the thugs, Ballistic, went down, it became clear how and why the Bastion of Bushwick had appeared with perfect timing outside The Empire State. As Fiorello moved on to the other threats, from high in the sky, The Whisper dropped down, flipped over Ballistic and bound his hands and feet with cuffs that looked like they had been built by a mad scientist, because they had been.

It only took minutes for Fiorello to prevent the damage that the thugs could do by taking each of them out. With superhuman speed and strength as well as skill that seemed to rival a Bruce Lee or a Jason Stratham: he turned all the thieves' powers against them until each of them fell. The Whisper had dropped from the sky and secured them.

When Fiorello finished his thrashing of the crooks, The Whisper landed beside him and the two spoke for a moment. The anchor couldn't hear what they had to say. He tried to approach the two of them to ask a question, but The Whisper without looking at him, gestured for the radio news anchor to stay back. He obeyed. The two champions spoke for a few moments. Then Fiorello ran away while The Whisper waited for the police to arrive with their paddy wagon, to hold the thugs till the Feds could get there.

Here is what the anchor couldn't hear: The Whisper said to Fiorello, "I am sorry to take you out of your city."

"It's the least any of us can do," he said. "You know you've only to call. Any of us will be here as quickly as we can."

"I try my best to prevent anything from getting far enough along that I need to do that."

Fiorello nodded, and then he said, "We should do this more often, mystery man."

"You think so."

"Together, she couldn't trap me in New York anymore."

"I don't want to risk daring Dee Spoils to make good on her threats for no good reason," The Whisper said.

"And I don't want to keep letting that stupid threat keep me from protecting more people."

"If I helped you go beyond New York, we would be putting people at risk."

"The eternal debate."

They left it at that. The Whisper nodded. Or, at least, the silver motorcycle helmet that he wears nodded. Fiorello left. In seven or eight minutes he would be back in the Big Apple.

The WHYY photos got picked up all over the East Coast and the anchor and the intern were asked to file stories for nationwide coverage on NPR. Papers across the country picked up their version of events. There had probably been a hundred other super villain crimes across the world that day, but the thugs weren't the news. A visual sighting of The Whisper, super crime in Philadelphia and Fiorello outside of New York - that was what made it news.

From the anchor's interview with Terry Gross later on WHYY's *Fresh Air*:

> **Gross:** I want to go back to what you said before. About the fact that the alleged attempted robbers you witnessed that morning were all "bruisers," in your words, and what you think that means.
>
> **Anchor:** There's a lot of speculation about that in law enforcement circles.
>
> **Gross:** And the fact that Fiorello appeared in a city besides New York, that's unusual as well? Is it not?
>
> **Anchor:** Not quite as unusual as super villains attacking Philadelphia, but nearly as unusual. Yes.
>
> **Gross:** And why is that?
>
> **Anchor:** Also unclear, Terry, and I can only tell you what the superhero bloggers say, but they say that Dee Spoils strikes any city Fiorello dares to appear in outside of New York.

Gross: And she's a sort of real world Lex Luthor, is that right?

Anchor: That's the word on the street.

Gross: Well that's ominous.

Anchor: If you believe it.

Gross: Do you believe it?

Anchor: Well, very bad things do seem to happen in cities Fiorello visits besides New York, yes. And, it is strange that a man who could run to Los Angeles in an hour is hardly ever seen in Boston or even Syracuse.

Gross: So, what do you think it means then, that these thugs were … I don't know? Poorly equipped to actually execute a major bank heist?

Anchor: A lot of theories are bouncing around the Internet, but I think in a situation like this the simplest explanation is usually the best. I think they were just eight dumb thugs who thought they could pull off one big score by hitting fast and hard and if The Whisper showed up, I'm guessing, they thought they could take him.

✷

THESE CROOKS WERE HIRED TO GET ARRESTED, The Whisper typed into his MonitorsNet laptop, later, the night he had called in Fiorello to stop the Reserve Bank of Philadelphia heist. His computer was a shimmery laptop with strange diodes and antennae sticking out of it. It looked like it had been built by a mad scientist, because it had been.

THE QUESTION IS WHY? AND WHO THOUGHT IT WOULD BE WORTH IT TO SPEND THE MONEY IT WOULD TAKE TO CONVINCE A GROUP OF THUGS TO GO TO JAIL?

He typed it up for a report that would be made available to all heroes in the MonitorsNet circle of superheroes and the team of private detectives and analysts they hired to read and follow-up on those reports. As a founding member of The Monitors he was fastidious about filing the reports. Though this one was the first he had written in some time that he could understand why anyone would want to read. Although his reports were probably the most widely read and discussed of any in the entire network.

If The Whisper's alter-ego had really had any friends, they would have known him as Ernie Weekend. That was his given name, but he hardly ever used it. He lived in an imaginary but effective Fortress of Solitude in Philadelphia's Fishtown neighborhood. That's the price he paid for becoming one of the world's most elite superheroes when a bullet from a .22 would hurt him just as badly as it would hurt the lady behind the counter at his neighborhood Wawa.

Ernie finished filing his reports for the night and he shut down his MonitorsNet computer and opened up his cheap Gateway computer. He checked his OKCupid profile. No one had replied to any of his messages.

He locked his sound proof window coverings and put on his Bose Noise Cancelling headphones and went to sleep.

✱

The Whisper had a series of regularly scheduled meets with liaisons from the Philadelphia Police Department set up around the city. He could show up to them or not show up to them. That was the deal. It gave him a way to talk to the police without giving them a way to track him.

He floated down to the roof of one of these meetings and was surprised to hear, as he approached, Police Chief Nicole Washington chatting with Officer Greenfield as they waited for him at their 3AM meet on the roof of Health Care Center #4 in West Philadelphia. The Whisper's superhero costume reflected his attitude toward super heroing. He wore a motorcycle helmet painted silver with a completely mirrored front glass piece so you could not see any feature of his face. He wore a bulletproof tunic covered by an extra-large long sleeve athletic shirt. The shirt was green. He sewed a simple yellow radar patch to it. Over the shirt he wore one of those photographers' vests with lots of pockets. The pockets were full of gadgets he might need.

He wore black tactical gloves, Army boots and bulletproof slacks. No tights. He had a sort of fanny pack around his waist with his gun in it.

It was rare for the police chief to meet The Whisper. Ms. Washington got straight to it.

"What do you think one of those guys costs for a heist? That one. What's he called? With the too big metal helmet?"

"I think he's called Exploder. Dangerous."

"Right, dumb, but total badass. FBI guys say he costs a crook a million dollars just to show up. And that's for a cake walk."

"Wow."

"So what do you think he costs if you tell him he's going into a town where basically no one ever gets away with anything? He's a dumbass, but I bet he has a calculator."

"Maybe the eight of them decided to try to pull a job themselves - without a mastermind?"

Washington ignored his question. "It's weird to say this because from what my counterparts in other cities tell me, the blind spot of you hero types is usually your egos. Your blind spot is your humility. You won't let yourself see," she told him; stepping close and shrugging her shoulders.

"What can't I see?"

Nicole Washington did something no one ever did to The Whisper. She touched him. She put a hand on his bicep and got close to him so he'd listen. She was a formidable woman in her 50's - she came off like the scariest algebra teacher you could ever imagine or like a woman who had busted some of the roughest street thugs, drug runners and bank robbers on the East Coast (because she had). You don't become the top cop in Murder City without knowing how to make someone maintain eye contact with you. She did, but this time she put a little gentleness in it. The Police Chief was worried.

"Whisper, you are one of the greatest heroes in the entire world. Even those of us in law enforcement know that the superhero community holds you in a regard that... well, it has to be a burden and a blessing. But unlike all the other majors - like Birmingham and Thunder and Gorgon and Fiorello - you just..."

"I'm not that powerful. I wouldn't survive a straight up fight with most super villains' dumbest henchmen. I know."

"And yet, you are everything - *everything* - to all of the Heroes. And to us. This means you'd really be something to the other guys, too."

The Whisper didn't say anything.

"Don't worry about calling Fiorello here. So Dee Spoils will hit our city now? So what? We'll deal with it. *We're due.* But you need to watch out for yourself. Those thugs weren't hired to hit the bank. They were hired to go to jail. God knows why, but we all know that. Something else is happening. Watch out, okay?"

The Whisper spoke but it was Ernie Weekend talking, "Okay."

He pulled out his digital camera and popped out a flash memory card. He handed that to Ms. Washington. Then he put a fresh card in and put the camera back. Then he did the same exchange with a digital voice recorder. These held voice notes from observations he had made and photos of crime scenes he had found. He was about to turn away and take off when she said, "Sorry, wait, one more thing."

"Okay," The Whisper said.

"I have been instructed to request your appearance at an event the Mayor is doing at noon on Wednesday. He's declaring it 'Appreciation of The Whisper Day.'"

"I have never appeared at an event like that - ever. It's much too dangerous."

"He has also instructed me to say that if you simply flew over it would be greatly appreciated."

"So noted."

Then she turned to the other cop on the roof with her, one of his usual liaison officers. He had been hanging back, saying nothing. "Greenfield, you heard me ask him, right?" The police chief asked him.

"Sure did, chief."

"OK. You didn't hear this next part."

"Sorry chief. Little congested, I can't hear you," Officer Greenfield said, grinning.

The police chief turned back to The Whisper. "I know you aren't going to do it, but please don't do it. It's a terrible idea."

"I'm not going to do it. Tell the Mayor that I'd rather he cancelled it. Make it schoolteacher recognition day or paramedic day or something."

"I'll tell him."

As he flew out to go out on patrol, his ears told him that the most urgent matters were going down in North Philadelphia. So he took a short cut over I-76. He flew above one of the many billboards the city had put up for arriving tourists. It said:

CAN YOU SEE THE WHISPER?
Then head the other way.
Philadelphians know that when they see our hero there's danger nearby.

The Whisper was in his warehouse one afternoon assembling a Captain Order suit for shipping to another crime fighter, this one in Dallas. Folks bought these custom made suits from Ernie Weekend in order to cover their tracks when they left their city. Headlining superheroes didn't need crooks to know they were out of town, but if the complex monitoring networks caught an image of Shenzhen, for example, floating above rooftops in Portland, then the crooks in San Francisco would know they had a little less to worry about back in the Bay Area.

So Weekend had designed a fully customizable suit - battle armor, really - that a hero could wear as he flew between cities and even as he operated in other cities, without alerting the authorities or the criminal community that he or she had left town.

The sale of one suit would cover Weekend's personal expenses for months, leaving him completely free to pursue all the wrongdoers of the City of Brotherly Love, but - of course - every order was an urgent order.

This was the sort of day to make Weekend bemoan his terminal singleness. He had gotten up, checked his OKCupid profile, found that his various carefully crafted messages had received no responses and then gotten on a subway train into Center City to complete some long overdue extractions of his wisdom teeth. The Whisper had no one to drive him home after the operation.

If he needed someone to come and help him battle a seven headed dog breathing fire that had just arisen out of the toxic sludge long dormant at the bottom of the Delaware River - he could have someone there in an instant. That said; if he needed someone to come snag him from the dentist's office after they put him all the way under for oral surgery, that was a no go.

Ernie Weekend needed to make that call - not the Whisper. And Ernie Weekend had no one to call.

This meant that he had gotten the local anesthetic rather than full anesthesia. This wouldn't be so bad, but for The Whisper's power. The Whisper could fly, obviously, but his real power was in his senses. It was a complex and subtle ability, but in the very simplest terms the Whisper had extraordinary, unearthly, impossible hearing. A normal person can hear the sickening sound of the dentist ratcheting a tooth of their own jaw, but The Whisper heard it as if his jaw were the size of Mt. Washington and the tooth were lodged more deeply than the cool crust of the earth.

And he could hear with such depth and complexity that he could all but see the sickening procedure in his mind's eye.

So then he picked up his prescription of Vicodin and took a pill in his apartment and was about to settle down to burn the afternoon in his Fishtown apartment, zoning out to his favorite decompressing movie, Michael Keaton's breakout performance in *The Dream Team*. He popped the Vicodin, as prescribed, just as he started to feel his jaw begin to ache and the local anesthetic wear off. Eminem had mentioned the pill often enough that he had thought it must be kind of fun. Turned out it was K.O. punch he hadn't been ready for. He was just about to succumb to sleep, turn of the movie and forget about the troubles of this world until the narcotics released their hold on him.

Then the alarm he had rigged on his PC to signify the receipt of a Captain Order suit came in and he had to fight his way back to wakefulness.

He walked east from his apartment along the sidewalk, to his warehouse about a half-mile away. He was hoping the walk might perk him up but it felt as though he were wading through glue. Then he got to the Wawa halfway and bought one of those big Red Bulls, but even when that started to take effect once he had made it to his warehouse the force of it barely diluted the viscosity of the imaginary sludge the Vicodin had conjured to hinder his walking.

He got into his warehouse, printed out the order on his PC there and started working on it. He opened up the Mayor's webpage and turned on the simulcast of the public ceremony that had just started at City Hall. He hadn't been planning to watch it, but now he was in his warehouse and needed something to keep him awake.

The Mayor of Philadelphia was declaring the day "The Day of The Whisper" in Philadelphia. Declaring it an annual day in which the people of Philadelphia would salute his work and all he had done for the City. It was nice to listen to all the nice things folks had to say about him.

He put the suit in a special locker he had built into the front of the building that only FedEx had access to, put in for the pick-up online and was about to let himself crash out on the ratty old sofa he had sitting in his warehouse workspace for years, when he got a ding on his cell phone.

It was an e-mail.

He had a personal message on one of the bulletin boards he frequented. The bulletin board was for enthusiasts of the classic first person shooting game, DOOM, the only one of the genre that he still really enjoyed.

It was a private invitation to play one-on-one sometime. That wasn't so surprising. What was surprising was this: the message came from a girl. She wrote that she had liked a lot of the things he had to say on the message boards.

She gave him a GChat handle to look for her under. The name was m4gic_ch4rm.

He felt himself walking home eagerly from the warehouse that afternoon. He thought he would e-mail her right away, but at that point the Vicodin finally overcame him and he went to sleep. He slept so deeply that he even missed going on patrol that night.

*

The woman who had emailed Weekend went by the online handle of m4gic_ch4rm. Weekend went by about a dozen different names online, but on that one *Doom* message board he went by Foggy42. They found a night to play *Doom* together. Then they played again and again. Before long, they were also chatting privately on GChat.

Ernie Weekend began to experience a sensation that he had not experienced in years and years - maybe not for as long as he had protected Philadelphia as The Whisper. He began to feel that he had something to look forward to when he went home. He would get back to his flat in Fishtown; begin filing reports on his MonitorsNet computer, but look over at his GChat status and watch anxiously as messages from m4gic_ch4rm popped up, begging him to play games of *Doom* with her. And that's what they would do. They would play *Doom*. He would frag her with the BFG 3000 and it would be great fun.

When they would chat online, she told him that she worked for some sort of Security Company that did research on people, for hire. Deep research. She described it as being something like a cop only she was sure she worked for criminals or at least shady types sometimes.

He told her that he did online marketing for companies from home. That he wrote blog posts and tweets as part of a much larger team of professional marketers and promoters.

Mostly, though, they talked about the Internet or about *Doom* and Weekend would studiously avoid talking about the real world or answering anything personal. It did not appear to bother or frustrate m4gic_ch4rm.

> **Foggy42:** Why'd you get into hunting for white collar criminals behind a desk?
>
> **m4gic_ch4rm:** I wanted an exciting career without all the excitement.
>
> **Foggy42:** You wanted to be a cop but you didn't want

to get shot at?

m4gic_ch4rm: Or walk beats. Or break up domestics. Or track down dead bodies.

Foggy42: Keep out of the glamour.

Foggy42: I get it.

Foggy42: Do you have a badge?

m4gic_ch4rm: Exactly.

m4gic_ch4rm: No badge. The weird thing about this job is that half the time I don't even know what case I am working on. They just give me a flash-drive full of spreadsheets and tell me to hunt for suspicious entries. I could be working on cases anywhere from Poughkeepsie to Saginaw.

Foggy42: So you couldn't give away any secrets if you wanted to?

m4gic_ch4rm: I'm not supposed to talk about it. They would probably get pissed if they knew I told someone we use flash-drives.

Foggy42: Ha ha

m4gic_ch4rm: You know, you are Mr. Secretive.

Foggy42: I know.

m4gic_ch4rm: Wow, was that vulnerability?

Foggy42: I guess I can at least admit to being cagey.

m4gic_ch4rm: So you're willing not to be cagey about the fact that you are cagey?

Foggy42: That's about right.

m4gic_ch4rm: I don't even know what you do for a living. I just know you have to write a lot of reports at midnight.

Foggy42: Ha ha

Foggy42: If I knew what I did for a living I might be able to tell you.

Foggy42: You know...

Foggy42: I'm just not sure if I'm the tail or the dog most days. That's all.

m4gic_ch4rm: You're not your own boss? I've always

taken for you to be your own boss?

Foggy42: Hmm...

Foggy42: No...

Foggy42: No, you know, I think about people like, I don't know, movie moguls and the Secretary of State... people with too much authority?

Foggy42: I think they are only technically in charge. That they have this whole machine that they are supposedly in charge of, but the machine is too big. It's too demanding. One person can't really run such big machines, so really the machine is in charge of them.

Foggy42: They'll never really see it clearly, anyway.

Foggy42: So....

Foggy42: So are they in charge?

m4gic_ch4rm: Are you Secretary of State?

Foggy42: Ha ha, no.

Foggy42: This is going to be sort of pretentious, but... Foggy42: I just find myself thinking about where the work ends and the man begins, you know?

m4gic_ch4rm: Does your work never end?

Foggy42: Sounds like you sort of know what I mean?

m4gic_ch4rm: Well, I'm not a <u>MAN</u>.

Foggy42: No, you're a P.I.T.A.

m4gic_ch4rm: It's in my DNA.

m4gic_ch4rm: Sounds like your work is very much on your mind.

Foggy42: Yes.

m4gic_ch4rm: But you don't want to discuss it?

Foggy42: It's confidential work.

m4gic_ch4rm: You'd tell me but you have to kill me?

Foggy42: C'mon. I'm humane. You'd be lobotomized.

m4gic_ch4rm: It's okay.

They went on like this for about six weeks. Playing games of *Doom* and games of who will open up to whom. She seemed to like him as a person to play with. She never brought up playing any other games.

She never made any mention of the fact that he wasn't writing on the bulletin board she had found him on anymore.

He never found anything by her on there. She told him in a chat that she was a lurker.

And he got scared when one day she sent him this message: m4gic_ch4rm: So are you on Facebook or anything?

✷

Ernie Weekend had never bought a suit before. He was in the Men's Warehouse on Chestnut Street, in the dressing room with a ready-to-wear suit on hangers with a dress shirt and a belt and some new shoes and socks and a tie. He had stripped down to his boxers and undershirt and looked at himself in the mirror.

"Philadelphia's great protector," he muttered himself. "The great superhero." He felt around his midsection. The great hero had a pronounced gut. His arms and legs were undefined. He had the haircut of a shift supervisor of an insurance agency's customer service department.

He was 33 years old. The night before he had orchestrated a six crack house drug bust bringing in more heroin than the Narc guys in PD had found in the last six months. All without ever coming into the sight of a single police officer or dealer. Though he did pick up one overdosing addict out of an alley and fly him to the front door of Presbyterian Hospital.

None of it scared him. Tonight, he had a date. He was terrified.

He looked at the suit the attractive sales associate had picked out for him. It wasn't really a suit, she told him. She said if he had a date he probably shouldn't wear a suit. But it was a jacket with some slacks. They weren't the same color. In his head, it was a suit, even though it wasn't a suit. She had also set out a vest, in case he might like it.

She had said, "The nice thing about a vest is that if you decide to take your jacket off it will cover up any blousing."

He had replied, "Oh, but I think I will just wear a shirt."

She made no expression in reply and told him that he should try it on if he would like to. The vest was made of the same fabric on the front as the slacks.

Now he was looking at all of it as if he were facing a complex trap set by an arch villain. His favorite approach for facing that kind of situation was to walk away and call someone. He couldn't do that here. Unlike every other dangerous situation The Whisper found himself in, Ernie Weekend couldn't recruit someone else to go on this date for him. He had to be the one to go.

He fished his MonitorsNet communicator out of the pocket of the pants he had folded up on the stool of the dressing room. It looked like a cell phone that had been built by a mad scientist, because it had been built by a mad scientist. He stared at it. Nothing. No notices. No alerts. Nothing he could use to justify putting on the helmet and floating away into some known peril. Guns and traps and insane mutants. Not a beautiful woman. Anything but that.

He started putting on the clothes.

When he finished, it all seemed to fit him okay. He looked like a chubby man in a discount suit. He walked out onto the sales floor and found his associate and said, "Does it look like I'm trying too hard?"

"You look nice," she said, "The main thing is that it looks like you tried at all."

"I'll take the vest," he said. "And… all of it."

"Okay," she told him. "If you think you'd be more comfortable, some guys are wearing pocket squares instead of ties for a little color these days."

Ernie's eyes went wide as if she had attempted to discuss the Curved Universe Theory from behind the counter at a McDonald's while he only wanted to order an Extra Value Meal. She smiled and shook her head and said, "This is a really nice tie you picked out."

"You picked it out," he said.

"You picked it out from the ones I picked out," she said, smiling.

m4gic_ch4rm had convinced Foggy42 to meet up with him at eight o'clock at one of Philadelphia's posh Center City spots, a super decorated restaurant called El Vez, whose trademark feature is a pimped out low-rider bicycle coated in fake gold rotating above the bar - with images of saints painted on the backs of each of the six rear-view mirrors. The rest of the space had been done up in comparable glam.

m4gic_ch4rm had also been the one to suggest that they go out and use their GChat handles as names. She said it would be fun.

He didn't know if this was weird for the current dating world. He hadn't been in the current dating world. He hadn't been in any dating world. Ernie Weekend didn't meet anyone and the only people that The Whisper met were cops and crooks and he never took off that huge motorcycle helmet mask.

But now he was meeting up with a woman for a date. A real date. That's the word she used. She used that word. She asked him on a date. That made it a date for sure.

She had sent him a photo. She sent it over GChat. It was a hi-res photo. Big. He downloaded it and saved it on his Gateway. She was pretty to the point of being intimidated. As soon as that thought crossed his mind he thought that Fiorello was probably not intimidated by pretty girls. She was like make-a-movie-about-how-the-dorky-guy-goes-ape-over-some-girl-who-is-nice-to-him pretty.

He hadn't sent her a photo. He didn't have any. Ernie Weekend had done everything he could to avoid leaving a visual record of himself in the world. It was a security precaution. It was also a defense mechanism against the way he viewed himself.

He did have one photo, but he couldn't send her that. It was more than ten years old. It was a photo of four kids at Day on the Hill in Lawrence, Kansas. All wearing KU sweatshirts. Two guys and two girls. The other guy had Ernie in a headlock and they were always smiling. It was from before the change. When he had been a normal person with normal abilities. When he had had some friends. He had it taped above his computer desk in his apartment and it was always falling down and he was always reminding himself to buy a little frame for it but he never did.

She told him it was okay to send her a description of what he'd be wearing once he knew if he didn't have a photo to give her.

So that afternoon at The Men's Warehouse he sent her a text message saying he would have on a blue jacket and a blue vest.

She had texted right back, >>Are you going to have on a tie?

He wrote, >>Yes. Blue and yellow stripes.

>>As long as there are no paisleys we're good.

He didn't know what paisleys were. He walked back into the store and asked the sales associate if his tie was paisley. She said there were no paisleys on his tie. He nodded, but he didn't text m4gic_ch4rm back.

And now he was standing outside, waiting to go in. Maybe she would like him? Maybe he would find a girl that he could be with for a while?

He walked in. The hostess spoke to him. The hostesses at El Vez are all very young and very pretty. He told the hostess that he was looking for someone and then m4gic_ch4rm was there. m4gic_ch4rm. She came out from the bar and a crowd of happy-hour types and took his hand and took over. She said, "There you are," to him and sidled in close and then said to the hostess - "We are ready for our table now."

The feeling of this woman getting this close to him was unbelievable. The hostess led m4gic_ch4rm to a booth in the far corner, within eye-sight of the El Vez photo booth, and m4gic_ch4rm led Weekend by the hand. She took him by the hand. That quickly. This was better than drinking.

Weekend asked if he could take the seat in the booth with his back to the wall. Which sounded weird as soon as he said it and yet he knew it was where he needed to sit.

M4gic_ch4rm said, "So here we are."

And that was it for Ernie Weekend. The date was over. He knew.

The Whisper's powers of hearing run much more deeply than simply hearing far better than other people. His whole brain is wired for sounds like a dog's brain is wired for scent. As soon as he heard that voice, he knew it, and it wasn't right.

He was sitting across the table from Karabos. A hero out of Atlanta. The Monitors had listed Karabos as "Out of Action - Unknown" for three years now. The Whisper had once helped her when she visited Philadelphia tracing a chain of arms dealers that had been moving military grade weapons onto the streets of Atlanta. She hadn't contacted him when she came to town. Karabos was very low on the hero food chain, but he had known she was there because he heard her working, and he kept an ear out for her.

The gangs had known she had arrived, too. They had managed to trick her into thinking that she was going to uncover an arms deal going down. It had been a trap.

The Whisper had gotten her out.

Then, Karabos had disappeared. Heroes do that. The life is a lot. Some folks find life gets in the way. Some make a mistake out there and can't face making another one. Some just go. Some are dropped to the bottom of rivers wearing concrete or melted down in acid.

The Whisper always encouraged any hero having doubts to hang it up. The cape was too much responsibility to merely accept. In his mind, a cape had to embrace it.

And no one was more honest with himself about the risks and sacrifices of heroism than The Whisper. That's why he had made himself into an island in a city of two million, hid away in his helmet, his apartment and his warehouse.

And now he was here with this girl too pretty to be taking a schlub like him by the hand and yet she was taking him by the hand. A girl he had, in a way, once known, pretending that she had no clue who he was.

It couldn't be.

Ernie nodded and smiled at m4gic_ch4rm, but he let his hearing expand outward. He let it explore the sky and roofs above him. Yes - he was surrounded. There were men with jetpacks and guns on the roofs of all the buildings around him. There were a few on the ground, too. They had him pinned down. That was fine. The Whisper wasn't worried about that, but Ernie Weekend, on the other hand. Ernie Weekend had to contend with the fact this wasn't a date. It had never been a date.

When he had gotten out of bed that morning he had checked his OKCupid profile, just as he usually did, and no one had replied to him. Instead of getting that pang of self-pity it usually gave him, he had looked at the photo that m4gic_ch4rm had sent and told himself he was going to see her that night. He had thought he had a date. But it had never been a date.

Beneath the table Ernie was tapping out a text message on his cell phone while pretending to listen to m4gic_ch4rm. He didn't have to look at the device. He mostly knew how to type a message without looking and his phone had a function where it would read back his text so quietly that even a dog couldn't hear it, but The Whisper could. He could hear it in the din of a noisy restaurant.

He had it right.

He hit send.

M4gic_ch4rm was telling him about why she had picked El Vez, what she liked about it, how they made guacamole right at your table. Ernie Weekend relaxed like he had never relaxed before. He ordered a cocktail. He picked out what he was going to have for dinner. He joked around with the waitress when she came over. He got m4gic_ch4rm to the point of playing with her hair, when he heard the footsteps. The only footsteps that come at the speed of 18,000 footsteps per minute. The Whisper could hear Fiorello hitting Aramingo Avenue, which made it about the right time for Ernie to say something uncharacteristically forward to m4gic_ch4rm.

"This is fun," he said, "but I would really like to know your name. Your real name."

She managed to smile and blush and pull back as if she were embarrassed. Yet the whole series of actions looked a little too rom-com for Ernie Weekend. Plus he could hear the way her heartbeat didn't skip at all. She was ready for this question.

"I'm having fun, too," she said, a little lower, a little huskier. She went on, "My name is Janice. Janice Janis, actually."

"My name is Ernie Weekend," he said. He paused. He made an enigmatic face. Then he said, "It feels good to say, knowing I will never say it again."

"What do you mean?" She asked. She looked scared now.

"You know. Karabos."

She frowned and then jumped to stand on her seat, opening up her purse. She shouted, "You stay right there."

A ruby scarab floated out of her bag and above her head. It turned itself around backwards and a red armor began to form over her body.

"You are really making me regret saving your life," Weekend said calmly, but his voice had taken on the tone of The Whisper.

The other patrons started to move toward the door. Janis showed no interest in them. Weekend was wrapping up his fingers in the tablecloth, and that's when the bar and the tables and all the stuff on the wall and the bicycle rotating at the center of the room all began to crumble and shake and fall to pieces. In fact, it looked like they were aging impossibly quickly. As if they were decaying. And one small looking woman with stooped shoulders, huge black sunglasses, long black hair and the face of a veteran substitute teacher walked out from the epicenter of the crumbling.

"Dee Spoils," Ernie Weekend said, as he pulled the tablecloth around his head to make a temporary hood.

"We have you, Whisper," the most feared super-villain in the entire world said. That's when Karabos, in her ruby armor went crashing into her so quickly that Spoils' personal force field was not enough to keep the mastermind on her feet.

The Whisper didn't need to turn to see that Fiorello was there. He had been listening to him approach.

"Get out of here," Fiorello said, "I'll meet you when this is done."

The Whisper nodded and flew into the sky. That's when the flying operatives of Dee Spoils on the roofs of the buildings began to take aim, but he's The Whisper, after all. It took more than superpowers to make him one of the very greatest ever to put a community under his aegis. He got away out of habit, but the evening left him so disappointed that he wanted to let the henchmen win.

Ernie Weekend was never seen or heard from again. The Whisper became even more elusive, while Fiorello came to cover vastly more land than he had ever covered before, and increased the effectiveness of his work so dramatically that the whole D.C.-Philadelphia-New York City corridor became virtually super crime free. This meant that several hundred other superheroes moved on from those places to embed themselves in other communities around the country and the world, making it even harder to make crime pay - even if you could throw a truck through a wall or temporarily stop time in your immediate surroundings.

It was the estimable public radio anchor who first posited that Fiorello and The Whisper were working in concert now. It was months before any other reporters could confirm it, but ever since his brief encounter with the two heroes outside the Federal Reserve Bank, he had made a study of the two men. First he noticed that Fiorello had dramatically expanded his famously limited field of operations. Then, he realized that The Whisper had not appeared in a single police report in Philadelphia in weeks, but the Charming Speedster was all over it.

"My guess," he wrote, perceptively, in a blog post on the station's website, "is that the two heroes are working together. The Whisper is the eyes and ears and Fiorello is the hands and fist." The piece actually crashed their site for a few hours as it exploded across the Internet.

Meanwhile, Janis Janice was sitting in Dee Spoils' Panopticon, looking out on dozens of former heroes and super powered thieves punching away at computers and putting their heads together, all part of the boss lady's ultra-dark network of spies.

"I just didn't think I would feel that awe again, if he wasn't in costume," she told the most elusive and dangerous woman that the world had ever known.

"You're saying you have a schoolgirl crush on that fat schlub, The Whisper?" Dee Spoils answered, pouring another slug into her glass of whiskey and fingering a file on a family of corruption fighters in Milwaukee.

"I'm saying I think I still have it."

"You came to me because you realized that you'd never be better than a b-lister with them. I put you on our A-team."

"You did," Janis replied.

"And you found out the name of the man who shut down Philadelphia."

"Inadvertently making us into matchmakers for him and Fiorello."

Dee Spoils laughed a low little laugh of satisfaction.

Janis said, "You're laughing?"

"Considering how we went about this… it's a nice irony, no?"

"I'm not in any mood for ironies."

"Patience," Dee Spoils said, "When you've been in this life long enough you'll come to savor its absurdities."

Janis ignored her philosophy. "We have his name, but it isn't any good to us anymore," Janice Janis said, rubbing the ruby statuette that once made her into someone people would turn to, "But that isn't all we know now. We also know that The Whisper is a soft little man. A timid man that can't get laid."

⭐ **L. ANDREA MOSIER** ⭐

A LESSON

A LESSON

In March of 2009, they diagnosed me with PTSD. The standoff with the student holding a .40 caliber Glock G 27 Sub-Compact semi-automatic was only a single event in a year-long fight to enter into the GAPING BREECH and deliver a little Shakespeare, a bit of Hamlet, maybe shine a little Pablo Neruda onto the situation. The situation being Inner City Memphis. After the INCIDENT, they dragged me before the School Resource Officer more times than the worst gangsters in the school to give chapter and verse for the inevitable reports.

The administration at my high school suggested I discuss my reaction, or lack of one, with the on-site counselor, who managed to complete an entire New York Times crossword puzzle while I unburdened myself. She nodded a number of times, suggesting that I come back if I felt overwhelmed.

Overwhelmed was not a word I would have used to describe what I felt.

What I felt was NOTHING.

She said that was NORMAL.

I was no rookie and had altered my own opinion of what passed for normal in public schools over the nearly fifteen years I had spent teaching senior English. Normal was not a word I would have used after my romantic visions clashed with cold reality sometime about YEAR THREE. Standing in the middle of my classroom trying to talk GLOCK KID down (Miles Vandiver, long, stringy, blond hair, somebody's son), you would have thought I had everything figured out. Listening to my voice, calm, the spoken word version of the contralto singing voice I once used in a church choir, the message was clear. I was in control. This is what they paid me for.

Looking at him, you'd think what a cute kid he must have been in baby pictures. Here he was in the middle of my classroom, a toddler in a man's body, holding a GLOCK like he meant business, shaking like a Parkinson's patient, snorting, crying, and screaming. I'LL SHOOT EVERY ONE OF YOU. DON'T ANYBODY MOVE. I'LL SHOOT THE FIRST ONE THAT MOVES.

I heard the air conditioner kick on. Heard someone sniff. I stood perfectly still; we all did. The twelve students who had managed not to get out the door when I told them to run leaned against each other, their eyes as wild as his. I told him he could shoot me. If he was angry with me, he could go ahead and shoot me. "But leave the other assholes alone." Or something to that effect.

The officer asked me if I had considered the possibility of a second gunman in the courtyard. I said, yes. The second gunman was a possibility. This one was a reality. Reality is the TRAIN barreling down on the intersection. Possibility is the car waiting to cross. That's why we were all standing here in the first place.

"Why do you think he didn't shoot you?"

I had a lot of time to think about this, run over the various theories. One reason- the idea that he was just another teenager who didn't want to be told what to do- topped the list. After I got over my gratitude for being left alive, it was the only theory I didn't throw out. As a rule, kids and people in general hate being told what to do, and my request for him to shoot me and do it quick fell on deaf ears just as much as "Stop talking," ever had, not to mention, "Don't make me come over there."

I didn't say any of this to the school resource officer. With Officer Buckle or Brewster I claimed I couldn't read the mind of a psycho. But the fact that such reverse psychology worked on the poor kid meant that he wasn't cold-blooded or even bonkers. He was just a fed-up human being with a powerful weapon. He was somebody I could understand. The sniveling cowards who failed to execute even one directive he gave them were beyond my comprehension. I had stopped trying to understand them YEAR THREE.

I had to go to court. After the witness statements and the depositions, DAYS PASSED BY. The first week, I slept like a baby, a hard sleep. Waking was like fighting my way out of a cocoon. Week Two, I lay awake to keep from dreaming.

The twelve teenagers he trapped in the room were like any teens on earth. Wiggly, giggly, emotional. When he threatened to shoot the next moving target, one girl started screaming. Another grabbed her friend and sobbed into the girl's hair. A boy fidgeted, finally leaping, screaming, and dancing around like a mental patient. I almost bonded with Miles Vandiver, THE SHOOTER. They deserved to be shot. They were idiots. Who the hell would dance around in front of a crazed TEENAGE GUNMAN nursing a death wish?

Ask Jimmy Underwood, the famed wide receiver of the Ravens football team. He danced.

When the cop asked me why I told Miles he could shoot me, I couldn't tell him it was just a long shot gamble. I didn't dare say that I was playing roulette with a complete head case, taking chances with innocent lives, throwing myself into the Volcano like some deluded old woman trying out for the role of sacrificial virgin. I didn't think Miles would shoot anyone who asked to be shot. Somehow, his life had gone spinning out of control, and this was his chance to get it back on track. The guy with the big stick has the advantage. He has all the marbles, you might say.

They quit making me go to the shrink after that. Right about the point that I really needed one, they cleared me to come back to work, in the same room, teaching the same kids. The first day, we all sat around looking at each other like passengers floating in the debris of a shipwreck. They sent a counselor to talk to any students "having difficulties" dealing with the TRAGEDY, but the counselor hadn't so much as darkened our door prior to the INCIDENT and it soon became clear that her presence was a matter of paperwork, the legal ass-covering to be expected. After a while, we let her come in and mumble her sympathies, give us a five-minute lesson on the stages of grief, and depart with our blessing.

After she left, a student asked if the numb feeling ever went away. She asked if that were the GRIEF stage or the DENIAL stage. I personally thought it was still the SHOCK stage, but who's to say? It all feels numb, like you're flat-lining, like everything died and nothing matters anymore. Glock Kid walked in and changed everything, the dynamic of our daily lives, our philosophy of life and death, but most importantly, he changed our own opinion of ourselves. We saw ourselves on the business end of that gun barrel, and nobody liked what they discovered there. We were all cowards, regardless of what we did or said. There were no heroes, just varying degrees of STUPID. Vandiver was right. We were all part of the problem, and he just showed up to prove it to us. We couldn't look ourselves in the eye anymore. He became our nemesis, only to tear us apart and tear off the façade, serving up our true selves as we really were, all the time. Whether we were looking down a gun barrel or not.

★

When June came, I ran to a dark and questionable bar in a part of town with the same reputation and drank until my toes felt warm and it took me a minute to remember my own last name. It was a stupid thing to do, but I couldn't get enough of incurably insane behavior, and this felt like the next logical move. I went alone, another stupid thing to do, and I waited two hours after my last (and seventh) shot of whiskey before I drove myself home. I stayed sober for one week and ran back to the bar. It became my Saturday night place. That was not only stupid; it was the worst thing in the world.

Because with human beings, patterns become habits, and when you make insanity habitual, the other members of the club start showing up.

Case in point, Jorge Rodriguez.

One night in late June, he occupied the bar stool next to mine. I say occupied, because I was drunk and could not have identified him in a line up if he'd robbed the place. Jorge talked a lot. In another life, he might have been a teacher. The good ones are actors, after all.

I squinted at him over my shot glass and noticed two things.

He was talking to me.

He was old.

He was telling me a story about crossing the border. I tuned in a bit when he spoke of smuggling orphaned children out of Juarez. They had to walk all the way to the Arizona border, meaning they walked the entire length of the New Mexico border to cross at a less conspicuous spot. There was a cave where they hid on the Mexico side until night when they dodged the border patrol. Jorge had a truck waiting to pick them up. The rest was easy. Any depravation, any suffering, was worth it, he said.

My sense of sight came back first, but hearing lagged a little behind. My focus fastened on the brass buttons of Jorge's Members

Only jacket. I hadn't seen one in years, and I remember reading the words MEMBERS ONLY repeatedly. The English alphabet is a funhouse trip to a person who has consumed seven shots of Single Barrel. After several minutes, the words made sense to me. Jorge was talking, and on another level, I understood that Jorge Rodriguez and I were cut from the same cloth. MEMBERS ONLY. We had the same problem. A bunch of lost children and no one to care for them. As a guest speaker once said, it may take a village to raise kids, but after the village goes home for the night, where they gon' lay they heads?

Jorge was still talking. "But that is nothing compared to the problem I have now."

I managed to look into Jorge's face. Brown eyes with a ring of stony blue softened a brown, weathered face. Jorge was not pretty. I was not pretty. Even I knew how it looked, the sad sight of a head-case high school teacher drinking alone in a bar with a rep for knife fights. It was useless, listening to all this. Like knitting with the streets on fire. My hearing came back and Jorge said, "There is a very bad place I must go. There is a chance I won't come back."

I squinted until I saw one of him. "Afghanistan?"

Jorge smiled. "No. I will not have air support where I am going."

"Where are you going?"

"To take pictures."

"Air support . . . to take pictures. Where?"

"I am familiar with this drug. They make it in Mexico. It will soon rival marijuana in my country as a marketable product to American Youth. The people I brought to this country were running from the drug cartels. The cartels move into a village, and soon, the village is turned to producing methamphetamine. I was a journalist there. I worked for my village newspaper until the gangs took it over. Since they couldn't write, they burned the newspaper office down."

"You Literate . . . Bastards. They showed you."

"Yes, they certainly did," Jorge says, taking a sip of his brandy. "It was a grandiloquent statement. An electronic journal, *Talk Nation*, hired me to drive up into the Tennessee hills and take pictures of crystal meth cooks, their homes, and their children."

"That sounds dangerous."

"Well, you know the drill. Whatever the Americans aren't willing to do for money, we Hispanic mother's sons do with pleasure."

"Meth families don't actually pose for photographs, Jorge."

"I am aware of that, Miss Prater."

"How'd you know my name?"

It hit me then, the way Jorge planted himself with purpose on the bar stool next to mine. He had come there specifically for me. To recruit me. A thought on slow boil bubbled to the surface. This might be the best offer I would ever receive.

"What do you want me to do?"

"This is your hometown, Si?"

A map of my home state swam up out of nowhere. I hadn't been back to the wide spot in the road where I grew up, not in several years. My more civilized existence I spent in Memphis, a place where art wasn't a dirty word and gay wasn't a sophomoric insult. You wanna maybe talk Infant Mortality, though, Memphis is your town. In fact, I was saying these things to Jorge, but the lag time between thinking them and saying them seemed like oceans of time.

I stopped talking and considered the map.

Big River. Smoky Mountains. Right where they always were. Near the center, a red flag marked a wide spot on the Little Duck River.

Jorge said, "I need a tour guide."

"No you don't," I told him, the words spilling out at a crawl. "You're not gonna visit the Bluebird, stop by Tootsie's, eat at Loveless. You're headed for hurtin' where you're goin'. They make meth up at Crossville, and I don't know that place."

"That's not where I wanna go. I need a person who knows Coffee County. Where you're from."

"What do you want with that place? What'cha gonna do there?"

"Take pictures."

"You said somethin' 'bout children."

"Yes."

"You're just gonna take pictures and walk away, leave the kids with the meth-heads."

Jorge tilted his head as if seeing me for the first time. "What do you suggest I do? Open an orphanage?"

"These pictures. They have a value. You do this right; they're political spaghetti sauce, fundraising gold, and propaganda, what have you."

Even I knew I was slipping out of teacher-talk mode and into the language of my former self. I had also spilled half my shot of Jack.

Jorge was talking again. "Yes? And?"

"Who needs photos like that? Who's it gonna help?"

"Miss Prater, if I might offer some insight. I've read the papers, and I do my homework. You came to my attention after the incident with the gunman at your school. You are the only person who can help me. I think you are supposed to help me, but that is for you to decide. You are from Coffee County, and I would like for you to help me find my way through its back roads and hills to several meth labs where kids live in toxic environments. The Publisher of *Talk Nation*, Dirk Landis, is a member of a Libertarian think tank. He believes that photos of meth babies will help him make his case for the legalization of marijuana nationwide. I don't want to be fired, he wants the photos, and that's where you come in."

"I don't know you."

"Landis will vouch for me. I have a mother in Leon if you want further references."

"When are you leaving?"

"Tomorrow morning. I will pick you up so that you will not change your mind."

"I haven't decided whether I'm going or not."

"You will go, because you will not get past the hostage crisis until you do something drastic."

Like come to America, he didn't say.

"Did you have a hostage crisis?"

Jorge smiles sideways. "In Mexico, we are all hostages, in a sense."

I thought about how we were all hostages to something, but I didn't say anything about that. I just let sobriety find me. I dug into my purse only to have the bartender say that Jorge had paid the check. He was gone, and the seedy bar turned ugly. Even in the darkness it had morphed into someplace I didn't want to be.

*

In the truck cab, which was filled with an assortment of clothing, receipts, fast food containers long emptied of their contents, and two dozen bottles of Aqua Fina, I sat watching the front cab gobble up the highway, while a Hispanic Country Music station played through the truck's sorry speakers. After the Tex-Mex station gave out, a hard-core country show sputtered and faded until it came in with a vengeance. A man sang, "She was stone, cold sober, she was White Trash, real back alley, she's a snake in the grass," and I knew I was home.

I knew we were going to talk about the INCIDENT as soon as the Saturday night hangover lifted. I knew, because Jorge was a journalist. As a species, they are naturally curious, and nothing beats a gunfight in the retelling.

Jorge tapped a cigarette into the ash tray, severing the long line of ashes and leaving the filter and a stub in his fingers.

His eyes still on the road, Jorge said, "Now, I am trying to understand where this boy went with his Glock Death Pistol before he came to your room."

"The library."

"They do love the library, those mass murderers."

He was talking about Columbine in Colorado. I was thinking about the drug cartel idiots that lit up the newspaper office in Jorge's hometown.

"You were under a Code Red," he said.

"Yes."

"A lockdown for possible intruder in the building," he added.

"Umm Hmm."

"So, he went to the library. I've seen the maps. The library is across the common area from your classroom. What exactly is a common area?"

The high school near the Mississippi State Line was only a few years old. The common area was an indoor hangout with Plexiglas windows, throw rugs, bean bag chairs, outdoor furniture, coffee tables, and a water cooler. Clubs could "rent out" the space for the price of providing clean-up and agreeing to replace or pay for any furniture destroyed. The first week, that's exactly what happened. Some idiot jumped on the couch until the bottom fell out. The female assistant principal smoothed the mom's ruffled feathers and the parents didn't sue the school system for not raising their kid for them. A couple of students got on EBay and looked up lava lamps and shell chairs, the kind they made in the '70's that came in lime green, lemon yellow, and pumpkin orange. An antique jewelry shop donated a few mosaics. The library flanked the hangout on the South side with the English department on the North end. After a couple of years, the Special-Ed teachers started using the space to drill students on state tests, and anybody with any sense stayed the hell away. These days, it was just a Museum to the Seventies.

All this I explained to Jorge, who mainly watched the road and couldn't have told me whether we were driving through Seminole, Texas, or Temperance Hall, Tennessee.

"There was only the solo shooter?"

"Supposed to be someone else, but that kid lost his nerve."

"The detective said Vandiver left the students in the library, told them to stay there, and ran straight to your room. Your door was locked?"

"Sure."

"The detective said Vandiver shot the door knob and the glass panel."

"That's right."

"He didn't hit anybody."

"'Cause I told them to run like hell out the back door."

"And most of them did run, but about twelve of them stayed. Twelve stayed, and I read that twenty ran out into the courtyard, which means you had thirty-two students in your class."

"Thirty-eight on the roster. But a few never show up."

"Why did those twelve stay behind?"

"Can't answer that," I told him. "Except to say they've been conditioned since elementary school to cower under their desks and wait to be shot."

"That's what the detective told me."

I noticed he didn't even blink at the number of kids I taught each hour. Thirty-eight times six was 240. I graded 240 papers every time I took up an assignment and said so to Jorge.

"You don't think that number's important?" I asked.

Jorge was lost in thought. "Twelve?"

"Thirty-eight."

"Seems a large number of students to teach."

"Seems, Mother? Nay, it is."

Jorge fell silent for a time. The highway rose in elevation, snaking between hills lacking in trees. After a few miles, the trees returned, long stretches of Poplar, Maple, and Cedar thickets, dark and brooding. Redbuds and Dogwoods painted the hillsides red and white.

"Hamlet," he finally said.

"Took you a while."

"I thought of it earlier. I just wanted to reflect on the significance. Vandiver's mother went to prison on drug charges. I was just picturing Hamlet sitting in the visitation room, and his mother saying, "Hey, Kid, why you wearing black all the time? You want people to think you're off your nut? And Hamlet would say, 'The nut don't fall far from the tree, Bitch. It is what it is.'"

I sat in the quiet of the cab with only the whine of the radial tires on the worn highway grooves. We were speaking the same language. I took a long look at Jorge then. He was brown of face. Like a potato left in the oven too long, the skin of his cheek appeared brittle in places, as if it might crumble in your hands if you touched it. His neck and breastbone peeking through his white, denim shirt appeared lighter, the tone softer. The sparse chest hairs visible through the open buttons showed up light brown. It gave him a fragile look, and I decided he was bi-racial. Even I could not escape the trumped up importance of degree in skin color, because it had been drilled into me back home in my rural school.

"Maybe they were psychic," Jorge said.

"Who?"

"The six who stayed home."

I directed Jorge to pull off Highway 41 onto a narrow strip that turned into a driveway. He stopped the truck and cut the engine. I lead him up a steep incline to a Confederate Cemetery. A cannon pointed at I-24 topped the hill.

"Odd," he said. "There is no graffiti."

"Nope."

"There was a battle here?"

"Here and everywhere within 150 miles. Can't throw a rock, as they say."

"And it doesn't bother you to be here." Jorge glanced up at the so-called Southern Cross, the Confederate Stars and Bars.

"I like it here," I said. "It's peaceful. Hardly anyone ever bothers you. Just the old white man who cuts the grass, and he real nice."

I was turning into Tess-Before-College with every mile. Jorge smiled and touched my shoulder, as if to make sure the woman he left Memphis with hadn't changed into some unruly, trailer-park baby momma. He continued to call me Miss Prater, which wasn't even my real name. It was leftover unfinished business from my ex. I was stamped all to hell with labels that didn't fit. Wanna get right down to it; TEACHER was the worst joke of all.

I broke out a cooler, and we ate egg salad sandwiches in the shade of the Nathan Bedford Forrest memorial marker. I dragged out RC Cola bottles and we drank those, too. Red hornets started circling, so we headed back to the truck.

"That was very good."

"It was breakfast."

"It is what it is, like Hamlet said. By the way, what was it?"

"Egg salad."

"Marvelouso."

✷

They had torn down the old general store and put up a Dollar General. The experience of walking the crisp aisles smelling of toilet cleaner bricks and off brand, fake cinnamon spice candles sent me reeling. As did the sight of White teenagers clambering up aisles, piling bags of chips, beef jerky, and Mountain Dew into a buggy. They all wore camouflage. One had managed to bring in a .410 BB gun, and he was using it to point out a revealing cover shot of Beyonce sporting a racy dress after the baby. They were laughing because Beyonce was past her use-by date in the unanimous opinion of all the young, white deer hunters in the check-out lane. I tried to keep my focus on Michelle Obama's image gracing the cover of Ebony Magazine. At the sight of the weapon looming between me and the impulse section, I nearly swooned.

"Easy there, Señora," Jorge said.

"When you gonna call me by my first name?"

"I don't know your first name."

Translation: *You're a teacher. We took away your right to a first name years ago. And, you're over 35 and don't need one now.*

I grabbed a root beer from the cold box at the check-out and handed it to Jorge.

"Where are you going?" He wanted to know.

"To throw up."

I did it in a square of newly mowed grass giving way to an empty farm field, and when he handed me the root beer, I drank the entire bottle in two long gulps.

"The gun?" He asked.

"Maybe," I replied.

"Let's go buy you one."

"Quintessa."

"What?"

"My name is Quintessa. White People call me Tess, prob'ly 'cause I don't give 'em an option."

Jorge stared at me. For the first time, he saw something other than Teacher.

"I will call you Quin."

I swallowed and felt hot tears, but I willed them back. I single-handedly stopped my tear ducts from operating. I had got good at this. When Momma called me Quin, I was not in trouble. She was calling me to dinner or to go shopping. My whole name, Quintessa Delena Verge, she reserved for discussing with me anything from grades to the length of time I had sat out in a car with That Boy.

I nodded.

Back in the truck, I wanted to find a hotel and shower off the smell of Dollar Store toilet cake and puke, but Jorge was using his GPS to find a gun store. Thirty-seven separate red dots showed up on the screen representing as many ma and pa retail outlets. Jorge found one close by and pulled in.

"Why you dragging me here?"

"Ownership is the cure for all fear," Jorge said.

The gun was a Glock model, the same one Vandiver used to change history. Jorge used me to buy it, because I could pass a background check. He bought ammo aplenty. I asked what he planned to do with his cache.

"Business," he said.

He took me back to the Confederate cemetery. We stood at the bottom of the hill. He pushed in a magazine and told me to fire.

"At what?"

"This close to I-24," he said, "You'd better fire into the hill. There's a depression there, probably a cave down there. Fire into that."

I did. On the right side of that gun, I felt alive. I wanted to shoot Miles Vandiver, but that feeling soon left, overtaken by a feeling of peace. A Zen thing, maybe. There was a devil in that hole, and he knew not to come out, as long as I was filling it with lead. Or, whatever the bullets were made of.

It was like putting fear to death.

"Better?" Jorge said when I had finished.

"Sure," I told him.

We drove up into hills until paved roads gave to gravel, and finally, a long dirt road running through a field of Hickories. Jorge pulled up to a shack hidden in a stand of cedars and shut off the truck engine. He crossed himself, grabbed the Glock from the glove compartment over my knees, and leapt out of the truck. He walked right up to the house.

When a man opened the door, Jorge opened fire. I watched the color red plume across the man's shirt, a slow progression. The man fell to the ground like a potato sack. Jorge whipped out a Nikon and took pictures. He took his time, getting the face up close, shooting the wound area, sweeping the scene so the lens could capture the event in full.

Jorge returned to the truck, tossed the Nikon onto the bench seat between us.

"What was that for?"

"Payback," he said.

"Who was he?"

"The Number One Meth manufacturer in the region."

"In Coffee County?"

"No. In Mi territorio."

I was pole-axed by this claim. My brain wrapped itself around the implication. I wondered what the dead man had to do with me, but I refrained from asking that question. Once again, a man with a Glock was calling the shots.

Whatever connections existed between Mexican drug cartels and Tennessee meth labs were lost to me. When day finally dawned, the sight of Jorge's gloves, my fingerprints all over the murder weapon, I kept my cool and stared out the window.

"You're very thorough," I said, not looking at him.

"They will never find the gun," he said. "But, if they do, there is enough here for reasonable doubt, no matter which one of us they like for it."

"They'll like me."

"They'll never convict. I will see to it."

"You'll see to it," I repeated.

We rode in silence for a while. He stopped a last time at the Confederate cemetery to drop the gun down the rabbit hole.

Back in the truck, I asked, "Who was he?"

Jorge lit a new cigar and smoked. "The important question is not who he was but what. That was a lesson, well-learned."

I knew all about lessons, lesson forms, lesson plans, lesson evaluations, lesson successes and failures. All lessons required a set of objectives, a set-up, materials, resources, a way to measure whether learning had occurred, and a closing.

All accounted for, in Jorge's case.

And in mine.

★ EDWARD J. STINSON JR. ★

DARK AMERICA

<u>WISDOM</u>

My first mask came from a pair of corduroy pants that I grew out of as a kid and refused to throw away. I used one of the legs of the pants for the material and dang near suffocated the first time I ran around the house with it on.

I learned a lot from that experience.

My first real challenge was learning that I wasn't as good as my big brother – I never had to be. He could do everything. He died when I was starting high school and my mother couldn't take it. She never really knew that I was there... she merely knew that he wasn't. She loved him more than me.

I learned a lot from that experience.

I didn't really need all of high school, I felt I was pretty smart, and my mom didn't care if I went to school or skipped; in fact, she really didn't care about anything. I didn't need a bunch of friends, I had comics. I didn't need to be home, no one missed me. So, I took some money, picked somewhere far, and decided to be a hero like my brother was. Life sucked, but I had dreams.

I learned a lot from that experience.

I enjoyed helping people. In fact, I originally intended on that as my mission in costume. I wanted to inspire others... especially the children. I found, over time that I volunteered more and did more good as a common person rather than in the form as my 'other' person; the costumed real life superhero.

I liked the things that I did to make people smile, but I loved the things that I did that were taking me to hell, more. I crushed the hand of a biker that pulled a knife on another guy for being 'of the wrong ethnic persuasion' as the others within the establishment. I left a drunken cheater in a bed of cactus outside of town naked; his girlfriend was fourteen, he was thirty-nine.

I carved the words, 'DRUG DEALER' into the back of a cocaine distributor I followed to the far side of town. He lived in a gated neighborhood and had two dogs. I couldn't get the entire word, 'DEALER' spelled out on his lower back so I left the 'E' out making it, 'DEALR'. I left him tied up at the foot of the bed screaming. I figured that whoever found him first would get the gist of my statement.

When my act was investigated, they described me as 'sick', on the news. They refused to see that he was worse. I was never caught for what they called a 'crime', but then again, I don't think they really tried too hard to help a drug dealer like that scum.

I retired my mask, my goggles, my jacket, and my tools less than a year after I started. I prayed for change and begged for help... all the while I continued to volunteer to help children, the sick, and the homeless. I got a small dog, met a nice girl, studied my martial arts, and churned away at my studies to get a G.E.D. I wanted to help. I wanted to inspire others.

I wanted to...

I wanted to...

I wanted to get back into my jacket, my mask, and my goggles... and so I did. I wanted to feel alive again. I wanted to feel that I mattered again. I wanted to know, that the garbage that I stopped was helping those that they preyed on. I wanted to be the security that my nation promised. I wanted to be like my brother.

I broke up with my girlfriend. I quit my job, and killed my dog. I had to fill the hole within me, which could only be filled through servitude. My brother served the people of this nation and so would I.

Through this I would find my purpose. My purity. My right.

My first kill was the scariest act in my life. It was terror, grief, and a detachment from reality that has yet to be repaired within me. It's something that I could share with no one and a time in my life that I found myself lying to myself about.

I learned a lot from that experience; for it was the actual beginning to my spiral down to becoming truly like my brother, my mom's real hero.

✶

<u>THE GARAGE BOY</u>

That boy I just saved was fifteen years old... and he wasn't a boy. He was just as scared as me and shaking just as bad. I'd never shot anyone before and I was sitting on the ground next to a man with a bullet hole through the bottom of his ribs.

He was bleeding to death and I shot him.

It was my fault.

It was wrong.

I was so addicted to the pain that I caused others, I could not see the control that I was losing. Breathing was even more difficult through my mask.

The boy crouched against the wall behind me in shock. He wouldn't say anything. His breath was short and each time I turned to check on him he flinched away from me. He knew that things were going to get worse, because the guy I shot had friends... and they were outside.

I'm not sure if I was too scared to reload my pistol of if I was too paranoid thinking that more guys would burst in while I was reloading... all I knew was that I called the blasted police twenty minutes earlier and they still were not here! I was too terrified to go outside and a part of me would welcome being saved by the cops.

The boy spoke to me really low after he noticed the American-flag patch on my jacket shoulder.

"A – Are you a cop?" He asked.

I tried to answer with confidence, but he saw the fear dwelling within me by my wide eyes peering through my face mask goggles.

My mouth was too dry to form words.

"We gotta go," he whispered.

My head flicked back and forth repeatedly as I went from him to the door of the garage expecting it to crash open at any second. It really stunk in here; my mask couldn't cover the smell.

I struggled with all of my might to wet my mouth and speak. I needed to answer his question and to give him an explanation. The only thing I could come up with was, "Okay."

My cell phone signal was weak and the battery was near dead because I spent the whole night patrolling and forgot to charge it earlier. I had some First-Aid stuff in my side pouches, but honestly, I didn't know what to do to a real gunshot wound.

The guy I shot was bleeding out all over garage floor and I didn't know how to help him. Heck, I wasn't even sure if I was supposed to or if I should. I couldn't remember how Batman handled things like this. The comic books left this kind of stuff out. I bet my brother knew what to do, but of course, he was trained to handle gunshot wounds.

"Hey," the kid said as he tapped me while staring at the bleeding guy on the ground. "We gotta go. They got some serious big guns and they're gonna kill us."

"WHERE ARE THE FRICKIN' POLICE?!?" I said to the kid in an anxious and hurried hush.

He responded, "They take a while to come here after we have shootings. We gotta go."

I yelped as quietly as possible. "I'm not going out there! I just shot one of their friends. They're going to kill me."

The boy looked at me then the symbol on my shoulder. His eyes studied me in the low light with his focus bearing on the white star on the black t-shirt beneath my jacket.

"You ain't a cop."

"Hell no," I replied. "Look I'm sorry about all of this. I was trying to save you."

"C'mon," said the boy as he grabbed the bottom of my jacket by the large star I had sewn into the leather.

He pulled me over behind the tool-stand on the wall and showed me a small hole behind it. We both crawled through and scurried over a berm and into the woods leading to a closed down recycling center. When we stopped, I had to pull my mask up to puke and breathe. The boy kept a look out over by the trash can as I tried to recompose myself.

A single pair of police lights... with no siren finally appeared in the distance by the garage. My cell phone signal increased another bar as I thought about calling them again. I decided against it.

The boy just stood there staring at me. "Who are you?" He asked.

"An idiot," I answered as I stood there on the verge of crying from fear. "I'm a dummy, a jerk, a fool, and I'm in over my head!"

The kid just stood there as I kept talking.

"I thought I could do something good. I thought I could save you. I thought I could be a hero. I thought I was tough by hurting people that did bad things... Now, I'm just scared as crap!"

He twisted his head slightly then looked at my gun. I held it up and that's when I saw the ambulance scream by and the flash of yellow tape going up in the distance. I dropped my hand with the pistol and looked at the boy in the darkness. "I'll never use a gun again."

We stood face to face for a moment longer beside the trashcan.

"They're gonna be looking for you," said the boy, "but, you saved me. I'll never say nothing."

"I killed a man," I replied.

He waited a moment more, and then said, "I gotta go."

The garage-boy then ran off.

★

<u>THE WRITING IS ON THE WALL</u>

I watched the news.
Nothing.
I read the paper.
Nothing.
I listened to the radio.
Nothing.

Everyone knew about the 'garage killing' but not a blasted soul cared who did it. They merely called it, 'a body found...' then went into how bad the guy was in life along with all of his crimes; after that, they nonchalantly went into the weather forecast.

I was scared to go outside... some hero I turned out to be. It figured it was only a matter of time before the cops would get me – it was only a matter of time.

I covered my gun with a bunch of paper towels, shoved it in a large plastic bag, and buried it in the back of my neighbor's yard by their tree. They're old, have no kids, no pets, and watched television all day. The cops would never check their yard.

I hid my uniform in a small cubby in the back of my closet. I was lucky. I won't be going out as a hero anytime soon... if ever.

It took a month before I started to volunteer again. I got a job, down in the plaza by the mall, fixing broken cell phones and dealing with attitudes all day... so volunteering with the kids helped me to laugh and have purpose. I wrote a letter to my ex-girlfriend and apologized to God for killing my dog. I was trying too hard to be something that I wasn't. I was SO stupid. I was trying to be like The Punisher, in the comics, and ended up discovering that I was more like Courage the Cowardly Dog.

As weeks past, it seemed that everyone had forgotten the incident and there was hope for me.

That was until a couple of months later when I noticed a spray painting by the park of a character that looked like my 'other' self on the wall. It had my goggles, my mask, my jacket and my stars on it. I dang near crapped myself.

I tried not to notice it or speak of it with the kids that I was helping during my volunteer service, but I needed to know.

"Hey, Terrance, who's that on the wall over there?" I asked in a casual manner.

Terrance was twelve years old, lived with his older brother and mother, addicted to orange soda, and his imagination.

"That's the ghetto hero that be around here protecting us," he told me.

"What does he do?"

"He's the one who took out Antney in the garage, way back."

My face went pale and my hands became cold. "Hunh?" I responded.

Terrance continued, "I heard that Antney and his boys were gonna kill a kid in the garage and ole' boy on the wall saved him. He kicked everyone's butt and blasted Antney."

"That's NOT true, Terrance! Where did you hear that from?"

Terrance paused as though I was disciplining him and I lowered my tone. I didn't like the idea of the story getting so far out of hand, but I had to be careful not to give away my secret. My skin instantly became clammy as I found myself telling him things that I couldn't believe that I was saying.

"Look Terrance, there's no such thing as real life super heroes or guys in masks beating up bad guys. That crap just isn't true!"

Terrance turned away from me and kicked the dirt near the roadside leading to the park.

"He called the police on drug dealers and wrote on the walls by the bus stop that he was watching over us." He then turned back towards me and said, "He's real."

"WHAT?" I leaned back startled. "What are you talking about?"

"He also bought Roddrick's stolen bicycle back and left it on his front porch, last week," said Terrance.

I became furious. "That's NOT true, Terrance! You're making this up."

"No, I'm not. I'm really – really not." He repeated while shaking his head from side-to-side. "He's even got a name…"

This is how I knew that things were getting out of hand; I never gave anyone my name… mostly because I wasn't sure what to call myself. I was debating between The Neighborhood Watchman, Captain Protector, or The Black Guardian. I wanted to wait until I got more experience and a reputation for myself first. Terrance just stood there anxious to tell me; I couldn't help but to ask.

"What is his name, Terrance?"

…

…

…

He smiled and said, "Dark America."

WE GOTTA GO

It isn't that hard to fix cell phones, you simply change the bad component. I fixed six bad screens, replaced a keyboard and did four full software updates before I had lunch. Everyone hated their plan, whined about their service, and swore that they should get a new phone replacement for anything under the sun that wasn't correct. My manager would have to step in each time to explain the policies and to get them to leave their phones for repair.

That was until Joshua walked in with his friends. His pants sagged, his plaid boxers showed, his gold 'blinged', and his attitude… stunk.

He threw his phone on the counter while kissing his girl and told my manager to change it with a new one. I looked at him from the backroom and asked myself the same question that most men ask themselves when they meet tough guys, "Can I beat him?"

I'd been working out three times a week and I still practiced my martial arts training from years ago. Heck, they even called me 'big- guy' around the office. My answer was pretty simple, "Maybe." It's his friend that I'd have to worry about; he had a knife on his belt.

The manager told me to change his sim card to a new phone, then disappeared into his office as Joshua and his friend walked around the store looking at other phones.

Customers began to quietly leave as I watched the brute slap his girl to the floor for saying some comment he didn't like.

My manager stayed in his office.

His friend went outside as he hit her a couple more times then came to the counter for his new replacement phone. I gave it to him and watched him strut out of our store with his crying and bloody girlfriend in tow.

I knew it was wrong, but I copied his info off of his sim card.

I figured it was time that someone made him pay.

Bully!

That night after I got off work, I parked my Volkswagen a street over from his apartment and crawled through a broken fence to the far side of his building. I didn't have my costume, but I brought a pair of my fighting sticks. I climbed up to the second floor using the fire escape and waited for the right time to attack.

I saw him in the room arguing with his girl while she was crying in the kitchen. It made me furious.

That was when I felt the rails on the fire escape vibrate from a faint knock made by someone below.

"Can I come up?" He whispered.

I couldn't believe my eyes! I said, "Yea." And the figure began to climb up to my location.

He was in an old ski-mask with a pair of lightly tinted round eye glasses on and a thin pleather jacket with a pair of poorly sewn on white stars near the bottom of it. He even had an American flag stitched onto the top of each of his arms. The part that really threw me for a loop was his t-shirt... it had a large yellow happy face on it. It didn't match at all.

"Who in the HELL are you?" I asked in total shock.

He scuttled up beside me, peeked into the window to make sure that no one saw us, then leaned back and said, "Dark America."

I was dumbfounded. "You're WHO?!?" I questioned, raising my voice slightly.

"I'm Dark America. Uh, I saw you park on the other street and come over here with those sticks."

Literally offended to be meeting someone dressed similar to my 'other' self, I instantly got an attitude and snapped at the masked man... no, more like, 'boy' in front of me. "Why the heck did you follow me?" I asked sternly.

"Shush," he responded. "You don't quite... 'fit' into this neighborhood if you know what I mean. You're pretty tall and big, but you don't fit."

I rubbed my eyes. "So what do you think I should do? This guy is a bully and beats his woman."

The figure looked around again then locked eyes with me. "Look, you don't understand how things work around here. This ain't a fight that's gonna make a difference. That's Joshua. He's been beatin' her a long time and she keeps going back." He placed his open hand over one of mine, clenching my fighting stick.

"This ain't a battle that you can win, sir. The cops have been here and she never presses charges. Look over there," He pointed down the street. "Those are his boys and they're all strapped with guns."

I looked at him and said, "Then what good are you, Mr. Superhero? How do you save the day if you don't have the guts to fight bullies like Joshua?"

"I don't, sir. And I'm not a superhero. I am Dark America and I'm just trying to make a difference in places that it will matter. As for guns? I'll never use them. I was almost killed by one and saved by one and neither result was favorable."

That was the moment that the masked kid became familiar. He grabbed my wrist and began to lead me down the fire escape. "C'mon, we gotta go," he said.

Once we got to the ground, he led me over to the trash bin and kept watch as I stuffed my fighting sticks into my leg sleeve. He grabbed a large potato sack from the trash bin and asked, "You feel like making a difference tonight, sir?"

I said, "Yea."

He threw me the sack and I looked in to see it filled with tomatoes. "Hunh?" I inquired.

"We're gonna go over to South Street to throw tomatoes at the johns pulling up to pick up prostitutes. It's embarrassing and it sends them home to their wives with tomato stains."

I could tell that he smiled at me through his mask. I returned his smile with a sharp grin of my own. He tapped me on the shoulder and said, "We gotta go!"

That was when I was sure that I knew him.

★

<u>PARK CLEANUP</u>

It was after they found the graffiti painted over at the bus stop, making the walls beautiful again.

It was after they found donated Christmas lights set up in the alley ways to make them less scary.

It was after the prevention of a dog attack by adding a chain to a broken gate that the owner was too lazy to repair.

It was after a beaten homeless man was cared for until the ambulance arrived.

It was after all of that, when the name 'Dark America' leaked from neighborhood helper into a local newspaper column as a 'Real Life Superhero'... and out into the world.

I hadn't seen him in over a month and yet I found myself driving through the neighborhoods every other night hoping to get a glimpse of him. I just wanted to see him again. I wanted to talk to him.

I found myself placing more energy into locating this kid, than repairing my relationship with my ex-girlfriend.

There was a flyer in the announcement box up at the church stating that Dark America would be at the park on the weekend for a community trash clean-up project. It would be his first daylight... public showing. There was no way in the world that I would miss it.

I traded workdays with Steven at my job in order to attend the clean-up. I had to work half a day so I didn't make it until the end of the project; there were so many people there.

Dark America stood in the middle of the kids as they ran around with full bags of trash, wide eyed with amazement, and cheers of excitement. Their hero threw the last bag on the pile by the road as the preacher shouted something with a grin causing everyone to chant strong gospel praise while heading into the tent they set up at the front of the park.

There was fried food, baked food, barbecue, and a major weakness of control as everyone satisfied their hunger as only a blessed community could. It was a joyful time.

Dark America stood up on stage as the preacher awarded him a plaque and spoke to the crowd. It made me pause. The masked kid

Trash

seemed more nervous of this attention than running around at night with criminals hating him. I noticed that he did a double-take when he saw me in the crowd which brought a smirk to my face. It made me ease closer to the stage.

I actually felt proud.

Out the side of my eye, I saw two figures enter the tent from the back with rifles. Just as I turned my head, I heard one of them yell, "This is a donation from Mr. Deal-R!!"

He and his partner fired at the stage hitting the preacher multiple times launching him forward into Dark America, as a bloody mess of a man, now gone. People started screaming and fleeing in all directions. They began trampling each other and capturing themselves in the sides of the tent forcing it to come to a strain.

The wood making up the stage jumped and splintered as each assault rifle round impacted it in search of their prey. The young hero was curled up in the back of it flinching with each strike while one of his hands was clenched onto the dead preacher. He was still trying to pull him to cover.

I tugged at the dirt and pulled myself below the bullet spray and stage deck then called out to the kid, "He gone, Dark!! We've got to get out of here!"

The kid was totally frozen.

The tent collapsed from the weight of the crowd as the shooters backed out through the entrance in an attempt to reload.

"Dark... Dark, listen to me, they're changing magazines! They're after you! You've got to get out of here to draw their fire from the crowd!" I said.

He just sat there in a daze.

I pulled his arm and continued to crawl towards the back of the tent forcing him to release the preacher.

He began to come to. "Y – You're right. You're right! I gotta go!"

"No, Dark... WE'VE gotta go! I'm with you!! C'mon!" I shouted.

We got to our feet just as the gunmen finished their reload. We ran through an alleyway, over a fence, into a warehouse, across a field, through a large concrete pipe, and down by the bridge before stopping.

I worked out two to three times a week religiously and I could barely keep up with this kid. It felt, like my heart was going to explode.

While coughing and huffing he asked, "Why did you come with me?"

I tried to answer, but found myself swallowing down air just to stay on my feet. It took a minute to a moment for my heart rate to calm down and my body to relax. "Because I believe in you," I replied.

The kid went down by the water and sat with his back against one of the concrete pillars while taking his gloves off. He pulled his eyeglasses from his mask and face then started to cry.

"Did you see that?" He asked without seeking an answer. "They killed Pastor Davenport for no reason." He placed his face in his hands. "I didn't even know them!! I ain't never seen them in my life... and... and they just started shooting everyone... shooting to kill me." He cried harder. "I didn't do nothing to them!"

We sat together for the next half hour just trying to calm down. I let him know that everything would be alright. We didn't say anything for the following twenty minutes.

Watching the stream below us pass made things better as his next question broke the silence by making things worse.

"Who is Mr. Deal-R?"

Something in me stirred from that question as I went over my own history and actions. I prayed to be wrong.

A KNIGHT IN THE PARK

The Park was as lonely as the night. The sky had no interest in the moon, and so its depth appeared endless. The mud collected within the boundaries of the park fence from the rain earlier, that day, filled no footprints because there were no children who had visited in the last two weeks. There was just a single set leading to the wet-wooded bench in the back near the merry-go-round.

It was a set that led to a twenty-some year old woman staring off into the night, named Donna.

She didn't hear the masked youth entering the park slowly to check on her. She didn't care. He stopped a full ten feet away and held his hands up and out towards her.

"Don't panic, Ma'am. I won't hurt you."

She didn't respond. Her eyes were soulless and her spirit broken.

The masked youth eased forward dropping one hand as though he wanted to shake hands.

"My name's Dark America, but most people call me, 'Dark'."

The woman was untouched by his presence.

"Do you mind if I sit beside you?" He asked.

Hesitantly, she shook her head a single time and whispered. "No."

The couple sat quietly as the night ached on to the silence of hurt without pain. The youth needed her as much as she needed him.

With his back tilted slightly away from hers and his shoulders drooped, he tried to sound heroic through a failing voice. "You shouldn't be here. It's not safe."

Once again, there was a pause, and finally the woman spoke. "Mr. Burbank died yesterday."

Dark America shifted his face towards her. "Who's Mr. Burbank?"

"The guy that lived over there," replied Donna as she pointed to the worn out apartment building cornering the park.

"Oh, you're talking about Bear. Yea, I heard about it. Y'know he was locked up for a long time, right?"

"Yea," Donna said softly. "He was in prison for twelve years."

"Bear was crazy, people used to throw acorns at him when he was on crack. He was..." realizing his brashness, the youth caught himself and changed his tone. "Oops, I'm sorry. Was he related to you?"

"No," the woman said as the darkness crawled over her eyes making her as anonymous as his mask made him. "He raped me."

The youth froze. His mouth dried. His muscles tensed and his understanding fled. He was only fifteen; he'd never dealt with something like this before. In fact, his understanding of sex was limited. The chill down his spine only allowed a single word from his mouth.

"What?"

The woman dried her hands on her jeans then repositioned herself to face Dark America who still had his back towards her. The park seemed even colder than a few minutes ago. She was a woman without tears. She spoke in a wavering voice as though she were crying. "I loved Mr. Burbank when I was young. I didn't know anything. He was the daddy I didn't have."

The masked youth turned his waist towards Donna and began to fiddle his fingers together. He didn't know what to do and so... he listened.

"When things... happened. I cried and I loved him. I said it was wrong. I knew it was wrong. But, I loved him. I was so young," said Donna.

Dark America turned completely around to face the woman then reached out and held her hands. She was taller than him and slim. He saw that she was an attractive woman who felt ugly by this secret. With his eyes as wide as they could be, he asked, "What happened?"

"I found out I wasn't the only one," she replied. Donna became as silent as her young companion who was still in shock as to what he had just heard.

He thought hard to himself then breathed in slowly before speaking. "I - I don't know much, Ma'am, but you might be blaming yourself for something you didn't do. He was bad... no, he was evil and he did what evil men do."

He dared to rub her face and said, "You're so pretty. You're beautiful. You just have to keep living and keep trying to do good. God loves you."

The woman smiled through the darkness.

Dark America stood up and stepped away from the woman then looked around the park. "This is my first time out in two weeks." He pointed at the bits of yellow tape bordering the edges of the park. "People got killed here because of me and I don't know why. This guy sent two people with guns to shoot everyone up... and it was my fault."

The youth fell to his knees as Donna came before him and dropped to hers beside him.

She whispered. "I may not know much, Dark, but you are blaming yourself for something you didn't do. They were evil and they did what evil people do."

She dared to rub his masked face and said, "I've heard about you, sweetheart. You're noble. You just have to keep living and keep trying to do right." Her eyes watered. "Keep being the hero that my son looks up to, Dark America... after all, he just lost the father he never knew."

The woman finally allowed herself to cry before standing up to walk away. Just before the nighttime embraced her as a shadow of love, she told the youth that God loved him.

★

GUILT, THE DEAD, AND AN ANGEL

If guilt was a fruit, it would grow on the dying tree of expectation. It would be nourished by the grim sunlight of failure. It seemed to be the only fruit in my refrigerator and hunger demanded that I eat it.

I thought about the shooting in the park every day for the last week and knew that it was my fault.

I thought about the looks on the faces of those who were killed and knew that it was my fault.

I thought about the masked boy playing super hero while dressed like me and knew that it was my fault.

I thought about the shooters...

I hated them all that much more than I hated myself.

I had to get them back; I knew that my brother would if he was in this situation.

It took a couple of weeks for everything to die down, but what sickened me the most was the news coverage on the entire incident - which spanned two-days, including a late afternoon talk show. For the last four days, the news had been covering a hit-and-run on the friend of the Mayor's daughter... across town. The girl was in the hospital with light injuries to her legs; the media felt that this was a better story to cover than the park shooting.

I became a source of rage.

I plugged into every phone that came into our shop and began a list of those who contacted one another. My web of contacts bled and grew from the ignorance of those who were addicted to social media. Facebook, Instagram, Pinterest, Twitter, picture sharing, text messages, video sharing… it all ran from the 'plugged-in' virtual world like a waterfall of shit feeding my fruit tree of guilt.

I saw phone cam videos of the shooting and the dead. I heard recordings that were shared. I read texts that gave nicknames. I saw faces 'tagged' online with funny pop-up boxes identifying the shooters. I read their real names.

…And the cops couldn't find anything?!? This was destined to be another cold case file within three months.

I refused to allow that!

It was nothing for me to don my uniform and goggles; in fact, it felt like 'home'. I left my guns buried in the neighbor's yard, but it wasn't easy because I really wanted to hurt these shooters. I needed to be careful because they'd already proven that they were willing to go to the extreme… and I never wanted to take another life again.

The first shooter was Justin Jones Junior; they called him Triple-J on Facebook. He was an hour's worth of internet research that resulted in a crap life, crap parentage, and crap decision-making. His apartment was a stink one room dwelling in the back of the local corner store.

By the time I arrived onsite to confront him, he was already dead. In uniform, I hid myself across the street only to discover his personal little crime scene in which he was the star. He was found in a wet newspaper trash pile under an old truck. He had a needle in his arm, a missing sneaker, a dingy coal-gray jacket with a cell-phone repair slip in it, and a pair of 'soiled' plaid boxer shorts; if it wasn't for the boxers, he would've been naked. I arrived in time to meet the yellow tape and to observe, the nonchalant officers smoke and joke as they cleaned up the body of the older-aged boy.

Weeks ago, I removed the ammunition magazines from the pouches on my war-belt and replaced them with other tools that would help me to become better at my new trade. For this, I whipped out a 41-megapixal camera phone that I had been working on for one of the clients at the store. From my location across the street, I snapped images of those watching within the crowd as well as the officers standing around assigned to the case. I wanted to leave nothing to chance.

I sat in my second floor hiding perch until the scene cleared and the night was on the verge of being considered the next day. I watched as life moved on all around the yellow tape. The dealers returned to their spots, pointing at the taped off area and occasionally laughing. The junkies visited them as gnats hovering around a sweaty man, the prostitutes whispered between the chews of their gum and the quick rides from their clients. The residents, who had learned to survive in this world, lived as best they could.

When I left, I changed from my uniform into my civilian clothes and walked to my car which was two streets over across from the park. I saw the most amazing thing on the way there.

I saw the masked young boy dressed as me in the park with a woman. He sat with his back more towards her than his front and they didn't speak much. I stopped in a mass of shadows on the far side of the park just to watch him. He wasn't out hunting the killers like me. He wasn't out taking down drug dealers or trying to stop crime. He was in a park talking to a woman.

He was nothing like me.

I watched him fall to his knees in the mud.

It moved me when I watched her follow suit.

She said something to him then vanished into the darkness as the messenger angel that she was supposed to be to him... and to me.

I just didn't understand why.

The young masked boy, that park, that angel, and this entire incident made me truly understand why he chose the name... Dark America.

The boy was truly good. Out of all the things going on, he knew what to do and I didn't. He sought an angel and found one.

I sought revenge, saw the dead, and found it.

I felt like crap. I still had so much to learn from this... kid.

★

<u>NICE TO MEET YOU</u>

Time is like a beautiful bug. It can pick at you and make you crazy or you can view it from the distance and appreciate God's wonder. The week that has passed gave insight, investigation, discovery, answers, and finished off with a birthday.

There was no mother to give him a hug or father to throw him a baseball, but there was a grandmother, a plate of breakfast, a kiss, a gift, and an 'I love you' to remind life that there was a sixteen year old boy in the world that mattered. He mattered because of his smile, his hope, and his dreams.

He mattered because he knew no world other than his neighborhood and the love of his grandmother; for him, it was enough. Their morning was warm bread, their conversation... butter. He held the small box she gave him, wrapped in old Christmas paper, and read the tag: 'To: Derrick'

He ripped into it anxiously and paused after removing the cover on the box. "Oh, my goodness... a phone. You got me a cell phone! Oh my goodness." The boy jumped from his seat and hugged his grandmother with all of his strength. "Thank you, Grandma!! Thank you! I can't believe you got me a phone."

"They had a bunch of old ones at the church and Pastor Jones gave me one. He said that it still worked but you had to get some kind of card for it or something," said his grandmother. She then gave him forty dollars. "I figured it will give you something to do with your day, if you went on over to that phone shop and got it working."

Without another word spoken, Derrick was out the door on his bicycle and impossible to stop on his mission to get his new phone working.

Down the road and across the park in the Theodore Brown complex, three swift bangs on the rail bars protecting the front door of his best friend's home had his little brother answering while wiping his eyes.

"Hey, Dee. What's up?"

Derrick responded, "Nothing, Terrance. Where's Craig?"

The young boy unlocked the rail door and let Derrick in. "He ain't here. He stayed out with his friends last night. Mommas mad at 'em.

She went to work. What you doing?"

The apartment was messy, but it wasn't dirty. Comic books and video games were as much of the furniture as the broken lamp in the corner and the three legged couch held up by a fourth leg made from a couple of old hardback books.

Derrick pulled out his gift. "Grandma got me a phone for my birthday. It's cool. I'm gonna go get it turned on today. I was coming to get Craig."

The kid's eyes expanded and he became excited as he inspected the device. "Can I go, Dee? Please. I ain't got nothing to do today. Mommas working and Craig is gone. Please, can I go with you? I won't get in the way, I promise," he pleaded.

Derrick thought about it for a moment. Then placed the phone in his pocket. "Go on and get dressed, then. You can ride your bike with me. I'm not going to be letting a lot of people know I have a phone either so you'd better not be telling nobody, Terrance."

"I ain't, Dee. This is gonna be cool. We'll be like Batman and Robin."

That summer morning stretched its arms and became noon as the duo arrived at the local plaza. This was the all-in-one center for those in the community. There was a converted warehouse on the far end used to repair vehicles, two ethnic food marts that clearly catered to either Haitians or Koreans, a 'throw-off' clothing store that was willing to take food stamps, a liquor store, a pawn shop, and in the middle... a cell phone shop.

Derrick and Terrance locked their bikes up in front of the shop and entered to find people of all types standing around waiting on service. Some that were browsing, Derrick recognized from church while others who were always in trouble nodded their heads at Terrance. The duo came to the counter and was instantly challenged by the short-patient employee with a name tag that read, 'Steven'.

"What you want?"

Derrick handed him his phone. "Can you get this working?"

The frustrated employee shouted at a kid pulling on a display in the background then inspected the phone.

"This here's a Samsung. It's not the newest model but we can get it working. You're gonna need a sim card, a new battery, and some updates. You got a charger for it?"

"No," Derrick replied.

"I'll throw one in for you. The whole things gonna cost you about twenty-seven dollars. You still want it done?" Asked Steven.

"I – I guess so… uhm… yes." Responded Derrick while counting the money his grandmother gave him. "Uh, Mr. Steven, how long is this going to take?"

"I don't know; let me ask our tech. Hold on…" said the employee before turning around to call out to the back. "Eran, I need you up here for a minute!"

Out of the back room a familiar figure finds his way to the front desk. He has a 'nerdish' presence and an athletic frame. His dress shirt is wrinkled with his sleeves rolled to the elbows and his tie loose. Steven handed him the phone and waited for his analysis impatiently.

"I can get to this in about half an hour. When do you…" The large tech paused when his eyes drifted upon Derrick. Both he and the youth stared at one another for a moment before allowing their next breaths to release. Their exhales seemed to be synchronized.

Interrupting the situation Terrance blurted out, "Mr. Daniels! I didn't know you worked here."

The tech reached across the counter to pat Terrance on the shoulder. "How are you doing, Terrance? It's nice to see you. I see you brought a friend up here."

"Yep. This is my brother's best friend, Derrick. Are you gonna be at the volunteers' party next weekend?" Asked Terrance.

Eran rubbed his head. "You know I will." He then turned his attention back to Steven. "I can work on this now, Steven". The senior salesman shuffled back from the tech. "Hunh? You just said that you couldn't get to it for a while. I don't want you screwing over one of our other customers for this project, Eran."

"I'm not," said Eran with his vision locked on Derrick. "I'm going to need the customer to come in back in order to answer some questions."

"That's okay. Just hurry up," sighed Steven as he turned his attention to another customer at the counter. Derrick ordered

Terrance to wait outside while he went in to the tech lab with Eran.

The room had a large U-shaped table in the middle with disassembled cell phones in all phases of repair. The air was much colder than the main room. Eran began to work on Derrick's phone without saying a word. He would pause every few minutes and look up at him, and then continue with his job. He recognized Derrick from the garage incident.

Derrick stood by the doorway with his hands in his pockets wondering what to say to this large nerd in front of him without giving away that he recognized him from the park incident and their tomato throwing escapade.

"Around here, they call me Big-Guy," said Eran attempting to break the silence. "I'm adding a sim chip in your phone that has endless minutes and uses my manager's code for access. It won't track back to you. I'm putting it under the name Kent Clarkson."

"Gee, uhm, thanks," uttered the youth still unsure of his situation.

Eran completed the install of the sim card and plugged the phone in to his computer for a quick charge and software update. He then turned to Derrick and stood before him. "I've been thinking of a name. I went through an entire list and decided on one. Tell me what you think of, The Black Guardsman?"

"Well, er, uh... cough- cough, uhm...," muttered Derrick before giving in. "Dark America and The Black Guardsman sounds good."

The large tech smiled slowly. "I know where the other shooter is."

"What are you doing tonight?" Questioned the kid.

"Meeting you wherever you decide we need to be." Responded the tech before holding out his hand. "By the way, my name is Eran Daniels."

His hand was met firmly by the sixteen year old youth. "I'm Derrick. Nice to meet you."

Both were anxious for the evening to come.

★

<u>WAR - PART 1</u>

"9-1-1, what is the nature of your emergency?"

"There are guys over here in the Jericho Greene Projects selling drugs. They're in room B-16."

"Do you see the drugs, sir?"

"Uh, no, ma'am."

"Then how do you know their selling drugs?"

"Uhm... they're drug dealers."

"Sir, do you need fire, ambulance, or police?"

"Police, please."

"Are they doing anything wrong, sir?"

"Uhm... they're drug dealers."

"We've had two calls to that neighborhood earlier today, sir. If this is not a dire emergency, I can't send an immediate patrol."

"Okay. Can you send one later?"

"You sound awfully young. Does your mother know that you're calling us?"

"No, ma'am. I just want someone to come for these drug dealers."

"I'll send a patrol over there, but they won't be there for at least twenty to thirty minutes."

"I'm used to that, ma'am."

"What's your name, son?"

"Er... uhm... Kent. Kent Clarkson."

The cell phone disconnected and its masked wielder went into action. The night was young and he had much to do before his meeting with his new friend, The Black Guardsman. He had to wait until his grandmother took her medicine and attempted to make it through her black-and-white sitcoms before falling asleep. He had to wait until the streetlights came on and most of the children had to be home. He had to wait until the predators came out and made the shadows his personal little fun place out of their sight.

Eran gave him a slip of paper when he left the shop earlier that day. On it, a name and address, Perry Ross, Jericho Greene Projects – B-16. On the bottom of the sheet was his target's nickname scribbled beside a poorly drawn tombstone, 'Pigglin'; Derrick didn't recognize the name.

His trip to Jericho Greene was a bicycle ride and a familiar destination. It led to the room connected to the fire escape where he met Eran. Pigglin was meeting with Joshua in his apartment. There were three other guys in there lounging between video games and quarts of beer. Things seemed like more of a party than a true meeting, but then again it was early.

Jitters crawled all throughout the youth kneeling on the fire escape. In his hand he gripped a small, rugged, dark-blue backpack with a smiley face button on it. He thought twice… and then thrice about his intentions. He asked himself if what he was doing mattered. He gripped the side rail and thought, "Will this help the community? Am I doing right?" Fearlessness would not allow an answer to those questions, and so courage had to step in.

The hand rail vibrated as a series of small taps at the bottom introduced his companion ascending the ladder in full costume. "Hey, Dark, I remember this place. This is that woman-beating jerk's apartment, isn't it?"

The kid somberly responded. "Yea." He looked over his new teammate and saw a short piece of wood in his hand along with a small camera dangling from his war-belt. "What's all of this?" He asked.

In what sounded as a shifty giggle, the guardsman handed a half-length bat to Dark America then disconnected his camera to take pictures of the people in the apartment. After a few quick snaps, he leaned back and whispered. "That right there is a short-bat. Bouncers use them to knock people out at the club when they get rowdy."

Dark America slowly grabbed the bat. "Hey, uhm, Black Guardsmen… we're not looking for that much trouble are we? We're not here to get in a fight."

His partner spoke without hesitation. "Trouble? Yep. We're going to kick some butt, Dark. We're the superheroes, remember? I've been looking forward to this all day."

"What?"

"Dude, trust me when I say that we can take these guys down. I'm trained in martial arts. I mean, c'mon, Dark, they killed some people. We need to take them down."

"This ain't the way to do it, Guardsman. This is gonna get someone hurt. We just need to stall them until the police come."

The Black Guardsman was stunned. "What? You remember last time? The cops came nearly an hour late."

The youth unzipped his backpack. "Look, I brought super glue to shove into their door locks so they can't use their keys. They're driving old cars." He then pulled out an ice pick wrapped in paper towel. "We can put small holes in their tires to stop them from escaping, if they break the windows to get in. The holes are small enough so the tire will deflate slowly."

The Black Guardsmen shrugged backwards. "Are you kidding?!?" He then sat before his partner and looked him over. "We need to kick their ass, Dark. People got killed." He then turned away from the kid causing the back of his jacket to fling up exposing the handgun tucked into the belt on his lower back.

"A GUN?" The youth shrieked in an odd and strangled whisper. "What the heck?!? Why did you bring a gun, Guardsman?"

"Because anything can happen, Dark. I came prepared. Let me let you in on a little secret… after you left, a text came across Pigglin's phone saying that Mr. Deal-R was coming tonight. We have a chance to get him and Pigglin at the same time. I'm not going to pass that opportunity up, Dark."

"It ain't right, Guardsman. It just ain't right. You shouldn't have brought a gun!" Dark became calm and softened his voice, "It's like you said… we're the good guys. We have to be smart. People that carry guns into a situation they didn't need to, often believe that it is their only option when something happens. We have to use our heads; after all, isn't that what superheroes are supposed to do?"

Moving away from Dark America to crawl down the ladder, the guardsman responded, "I am using my head, Dark. Those guys carry guns, too. I'm not going to let them get away. There's a time to fight and there's a time to run. I'm not running from this fight. I'm going to be a hero, just like my brother!"

He then slid down the ladder. "You can go take care of the cars and whatever, I'm going around the building to bust in and make a citizen's arrest." The Black Guardsmen disappeared into the shadows.

★

<u>WAR – PART 2</u>

Dark America stood frozen in confusion for a moment then dashed down the fire escape, through the alley, and out to the shadowed edges of the parked cars in front of the complex. There were people across the street hanging out and playing music; the young guys, selling drugs, the young girls, selling themselves. The only one that seemed to notice or much less care about a masked boy squeezing super glue into the door locks of two old cars, was a mangy dog feeding out of an old paper bag beside a homeless man. The dog stared for all but a moment, and then stuffed his face back into the bag.

The masked boy moved along the shadows to each tire, puncturing them with his ice pick. He saw the Black Guardsman on the far side of the building, looking up with his back against the wall and his gun drawn; he was praying.

"Oh my god," whispered Dark America. His mind began to rush through his memories as his internal fear sought confirmation. He had glimpses of his grandmother and her worries. He had glimpses of Terrance and his laughter. He had glimpses of Craig, his best friend and Terrance's older brother... who wanted revenge for being beaten up at school.

Craig wanted a gun. He thought the gun would fix things.

It was Derrick that confronted Antney before he could sell the gun to Craig. It was Derrick who was beaten in an old repair shop garage while Antney's crew stood outside. It was Derrick who met fear and saw death. It was that night he was saved by the Black Guardsmen.

He knew that tonight, he would have to return the favor. His fear was confirmed.

The Black Guardsmen seemed to inhale before thrusting himself through the apartment complex doors and up the stairs into the unknown. Dark America followed him and paused at the base of the stairs as his legs became weak. Feared overwhelmed him and each step up became a mountain that he had to climb.

Derrick was a 16 year old boy who knew about the streets but lived in the world of heroes and hope. He did not see himself as a 'super' hero but instead as a helper; he just wanted to do good things. The kicking in of the door upstairs made his shoulders jump and sent a chill through him.

A muffled voice was heard. "Who the hell are you?!?"

"Shut up, Joshua! I'm here for Pigglin!" Shouted the guardsman as his voice echoed through the hallway.

There were more shouts and scuffling as neighbors began to peek out into the hallway. For Dark America, he had barely made it to the fourth step.

Shouts became screams as the commotion took a grim turn into fighting, struggle, and an all-too-familiar shot. The crack of the weapon was not as piercing as expected but more of a snap that felt like a wasp stinging one's soul. Dark America pulled himself forward to the top of the stairs as his breathing became as shallow and swift as his heartbeat.

Three more shots rang out into the poorly lit area showcasing the brightness from the doorway where the disturbance was home.

Someone bellowed, "HELP ME..." as furniture crashed into the walls and glass shattered. The sound of two more shots blasted from the room and multiple shrieks could be heard followed by people collapsing and groaning.

Dark America had finally made it to the doorway of the room.

Inside, Pigglin lay dead in the center of the room with a gunshot wound to his head, while Joshua was curled up in the kitchen barely breathing with his stomach running blood and bodily fluids all over the floor. His gun was a pitch away from him by the table. The other three guys were all dead with two having shots in their backs and the final one, a point blank shot in the back of his head.

On top of Pigglin, the Black Guardsmen laid face down with his gun loosely held in his hand. Dark America ran over to him. "No... No... NO! Eran!" He turned him over on his back and lurched away in shock as he saw the entry point of his bullet wound through his collar bone and into his neck. Blood spurted with each of his poorly taken breaths.

"I – I don't know what to do. Eran, I don't know what to do!" Cried Dark as he pressed his hands against the guardsman's neck. He could see his eyes, barely open, through his goggles as they looked up at him. Dark America pulled his mask off and then off of his friend, "Tell me what to do, Eran. Please, don't die… please."

Eran could barely speak as his bloodshot eyes rolled up against his will. He fought with his remaining strength to focus on Dark America.

"Y – You were right," he whispered through globs of blood. "T – Tell my mama…"

Eran became limp as his final battle for focus became failure; death had found its place. Dark America began to tremble and shake as he cried while holding the person who had saved his life. He then became silent and replaced both his and his friend's mask.

Knowing that the police would be coming, Dark decided to exit through the window leading to the fire escape. He grabbed the camera from the guardsmen belt and began to crawl through the window when he heard someone else barging up the stairs and enter the hallway outside of the doorway to the room.

"You son-of-a-bitch! I'm gonna kill you!" Shouted an older man hastily bringing up a shotgun to fire. Dark turned around just as the shotgun blast went off destroying the bookshelf beside him and clipping his backpack. It shoved him into the rails of the fire escape.

A new series of gunshots ringed out as the old man danced chaotically from a rain of bullet impacts. His legs stiffened as his torso jerked in an unnatural twist forcing his body to drop in a sudden clump of death. Dark America watched from the corner of the fire escape as two police officers raced to the top of the stairs to examine the man's body. That was his queue to leave as he vanished into the alleyways below.

EPILOGUE

The next day the local and national news stations reported the incident and called it the 'Jericho Shootout'. It was reported that the police, responding to an anonymous call, encountered a well-known narcotics distributor in the hallways of the Jericho Projects apartments. The suspect fired his weapon and the police returned fire, fatally wounding him. The suspect was later identified as one Levin Andersen Martin. He was known throughout the underground as, 'Mr. Deal-R' because of a set of knife scars on his back made by a masked man that invaded his home a year earlier.

There was a single survivor, Joshua, whom the police had in custody; he was in a coma. The other bodies found in the apartment were identified with very little emphasis on their importance, that is, all except for the one known as 'Pigglin', Perry Ross and the masked shooter, who was described as a hero by those in the community and a vigilante by law enforcement.

Eran Daniels was identified as the younger brother of Kenneth Daniels, a Navy corpsman stationed in Afghanistan. Kenneth, allegedly, killed three guys in his squad, then entered his commander's tent, killed him and shot himself. He left a note describing a raping and killing of a young Afghan girl and her family. None of it was proven – the government denied the incident and stated that Kenneth was experiencing symptoms of PTSD. His mother took his death extremely hard and lost herself to alcohol.

Kenneth's younger brother Eran had created an entire string of shows, discussions, spotlights, and studies into Real Life Superheroes. The images on the walls all throughout the neighborhood displayed the communities love for him as more and more drawings created by fans poured in from all over the nation to a website dedicated to him. Eran became famous in death. He became a debatable inspiration to other costumed heroes as they attempted to follow in his footsteps.

He became what America wanted and feared. Eran Daniels became what he was called, by the ignorant, in the newspaper. He became Dark America.

And out of all of this, there was no mention of Derrick.

★ SUZANNIE M. LAWRENCE ★

FOR THE HONOR OF STROMGARD

"So I ram my fist into his gullet and I swear by the thief Godren Renh, he just stood there like a fly landed on him. Scared me, he did."

The gruff looking man grabs his tankard of ale and after guzzling several swallows, slams the tankard down splashing ale over the beefcake, loaf of bread, hardened cheese, and men sitting around the table. He wipes the back of his hand across his unkempt face, the food and drink left to mingle in his dirty red beard.

"Not as tough as you make out to be, huh, Otto." Burping, one of the drunken men jokes as he wipes the spilled ale off the front of his shirt.

"Stuff it, you cutthroat, you not as tough as you make out to be either, Keros. Rumor is your own woman slaps you about every so often." Otto smacks his leg and lets out a loud laugh as the other three men in attendance join in laughter at their drinking partner.

As the drunken man staggers to his feet, he pulls up his breeches and brandishes his insulted ego.

"I don't let a woman lay a hand on me unless she's going to give me some sort of pleasure." He grabs his crotch, slurring his speech and spitting ale. "No one takes me on. None of you ever took me and none in this dump can either." He flings his arms around the entirety of the room, causing him to tilter off balance.

The barmaid and innkeeper both give a quick glance at the boastful man as he speaks and staggers. Glancing around, he sees the few patrons in the bar give him a quick glance while trying to avoid eye contact and the invitation of a brawl. He pulls his pants up as he spins on his heels trying not to fall over. A broad smile on his face, he looks at his companions.

"See, every one of 'em. Back down they did, can't even stomach to look me in the eye too long." Keros swings his arm again to span the bar and its patrons, stopping as a cloaked figure sits in the far corner with two men, paying no attention to his triumphant display.

"Yea, you really scared 'em into backing down Keros." Otto admits as he uses his dagger to cut a chunk of bread.

"Hey, I think I might have found a challenger." Keros announces loudly with his back turned to his companions.

Otto leans left, looking around the drunken Keros to observe three men hidden in the shadowed part of The Feathered Horse Inn.

"Ah, leave 'em be Keros, they look like nothing more than traveling merchants, hoping to squeeze a few coins out of the cities pockets like us." Otto stuffs the bread into his mouth and washes it down with more ale. "By the looks of that..." Otto scantily finishes his sentence when Keros advances towards the men.

"Hey! You think you can take me?" Keros asks now standing behind the seated cloaked man, the other two sitting, not looking up. "You heard me." Keros pushes the man's shoulder, nudging him forward causing him to spill some of his drink.

The sound of the wooden chairs sliding back and two men suddenly on their feet ready to act are stilled by a raised hand of the cloaked figure.

"It's alright," the man speaks. "I'm sure this is a misunderstanding. This fellow wants no trouble." His voice deep and commanding, even in its low tone.

The two armed men slowly sit down in chorus with the cloaked man's lowering hand. Their face masked with vigilance, of Keros as well as his companions.

Keros backs up slightly and laughs. "You think yourself my better, to be commanding men with your hand and telling me what's what." Keros yells and the unsheathing of his sword sings a deadly hymn in unison with his voices pitch and tone.

His companion's weapons are drawn and they are at his back and ready to meet any challenge from the three men.

"Why are you drunks always causing trouble here?" A stern feminine voice breaks the tension as the cloaked man finally stands, and he turns with his men to face Keros and his band of cutthroats.

A tall statuesque woman emerges from the kitchen, holding a tray of fresh baked pastries, steam rising off the rolls, the melted caramel swirls matching her flawless skin and the white powdered sugar dusted over the caramel swirls, sprinkled on her pink blouse. She moves across the floor with elegant grace as the men all pause, allowing her to pass between them and set the rolls on the table of the cloaked man.

"Here is your order, sir. Will you require more ale as well?" She says politely and slowly backs away from the table.

"You're one of the instructors at the academy," the shrouded figure states, not as a question, but a statement, she notices.

She turns her head to him. "Yes, I am Headmistress Shar Chrystel. And you sir, regardless of who you are, you are about to be expelled from my establishment," she says smiling brazenly at him.

"I'm just here for The Feathered Horse Inn's Caramel Rolls. They are served nowhere else in Saenia I hear."

"What's this? Are you here to woo the bitch or are you going to prove you can best me, pretty man," Keros intrudes, and proceeded to slice his sword through the air between Shar and the man.

Abruptly and with a flash of blinding red light, Keros and his men are flung back and sent flying across the inn, crashing into their drinking table and chairs. The five men fall over food and broken wood as they stumble only to fall again, shaken from the jolt of the magical blast of a Mystic's Mage power.

The commotion clears several of the patrons from the inn's small dining area and bar.

"I know you!" Shar says to the hooded man as she turns her attention back to the cutthroat, her hands extended and fingers fanned out.

As the men gather themselves and ready their blades for the melee, Shars' fingers begin to glow a soft red and the spell forms.

"She's a Sigil!" Otto spits the words to Keros.

Keros tugs at his sword belt and takes a fighting stance, parting his legs as he brings his sword down ready for a fight.

"You've no idea when to back down you drunken swine. You insane? Look about you Keros, two of our men, knocked out, we're too drunk to piss straight and you want to take on a Sigil and three well-armed men?"

Keros sneers at Otto and grabs the man by his shirt collar, pulling him close to his face.

"No one dishonors me." Keros insists.

Otto pulls back as spit flies into his face and the foul breath of his friend stings his nostrils.

"We're thieves, not men of honor. What's honor to men like us?

We've no honor 'an we ain't ask for none. You'd be wise to 'member how we survived this long in the world." Otto stands firm against the drunken anger of his companion.

Keros' anger, at its peak, makes the drunken man unreasonable to his companion's words. He pushes forward into Otto's chest ready to challenge him, as his other companions stagger to their feet.

"If you insist to try claiming what wasn't yours in the first place." Otto sheathes his sword and takes a side step. "Go... claim your honor, idiot!"

The other companions stand unmoved.

Shar stands firm. Her extended arms ready for the fight with the two armed men at her side.

The shrouded man, his hand resting on his sword hilt standing behind them, moves up and rest a gentle hand on the Mystics arm, interrupting her spell casting. Her spell's manna draining slowly, now replenishing her essence.

"That won't be necessary Headmistress Chrystel." He steps forward pulling his hood back to reveal his face and curly light brown hair. As he walks toward the pair of bickering men, Otto's eyes squint.

"You look..." Otto's jaw drops as realization sets in when he closely observes the two sentinels standing next to the Headmistress, now that their cloaks have parted and given him a better view of their uniforms. He now notices the fine, although simple shirt worn by the man. He grabs at Keros just as the belligerent man's stride opens up. "This ain't worth the dungeon or execution."

"What are you rambling about, fool?"

Otto steps out in front. "My Liege, pardon. The ale dulled our senses."

Keros looks around confused, but silent. Shar smiles devilishly at the man's embarrassment. King Garras Youngstrom of Saenia, steps forward, his Sentinels taking their place at his side.

"You men are a boastful lot, eh? For a group of thieves and cutthroats, you want to pride yourself in having honor only when it suits you it seems," King Garras says moving closer to them.

"Where is the honor in thrusting your blade in some patron's gut when your mind and vision has been drowned in a haze of ale?" He gestures towards the blade in Keros' hand then points directly to him to emphasize the statement.

"Did you feel that passion that burned in your heart when you thought someone challenged you? The rage in your soul that made you ready to fight three well-armed men and a trained Sigil even if you knew you might not survive the ordeal?" He says pounding his chest with his hand, letting the thud of it send shivers through those witnessing.

"That is the zeal we need in this time of conflict in our kingdom. Surely you've heard of the happenings throughout the realm?" Garras says as his face twists with the pain from the thought of the war his land is suffering from.

"The lives you live, full of thievery and surviving off the money gained from threatening innocent people... That's not a life worth living. There is no honor. No pride. No gain. It becomes simply, waking up to another day of suffering and scavenging off of those as poor or less fortunate than you." He paces as he speaks, with Shar and his Sentinels at ease behind him and Keros along with his companions staying enthralled by their King's words.

"You are men who see only the present and survival in the present. I see greater. I see a potential in each of you."

Garras' eyes look into Keros, past his vision and into his soul.

Keros lowers his head a bit as he feels a strange sensation of guilt.

"Keros, I see in you, the ability to lead men from the front. The courage to gain the trust of others and bring out the vigor in them."

He turns to Otto.

"You, I see the eyes of a man who will keep his allies humbled. I see a man who can be of wisdom and of word in times of stressful conflict."

The king moves a hand's grasp away from Keros. Keros' sword arm goes limp as he is hypnotized by his king's voice.

"Use these natural abilities for good in our army. You scour the streets and alleyways for scraps of food left out by others. What coin you rob, you squander on ale. Trying to drown your shame. Leave that behind you. In your kingdom's army you are lodged and armed and protected by the brothers-at-arms who stand by your side and fight for the same cause you fight for." Garras stops, his face becoming stern. "Earn the respect and honor you seek. Earn the chance to serve your land and its people. Those same people, who look at you now in fear and disgust, can look at you with pride and admiration. Be better men! Serve Stromgard's army! Become the heroes this land needs," Garras says finishing, his voice loud and commanding, and his eyes on Keros.

Keros and his men glance at each other and then at the few people left in The Feathered Horse Inn. His jaw tightens as does his fist.

Otto breaks the silence.

"The Godren Renh has never gotten me nothing but bad luck and jail time for what's to have been easy pickings." The man turns his head and spits on the ground as he wrinkles his face and grits his teeth. "You're our king, true, and I admit we never paid the respect due the royals. I never thought much of the city's problems. I never thought much of how we are one of the city's problems." Otto rubs his rough hand over his face, ending with him pulling on his dirty red beard. He turns to face his companions. "What say we try it? It's honor and respect we seek, and if we can get it while we're paid... ain't no harm in doin it."

Keros and the rest of the men gather and sheath their weapons. They look at their king, nodding at the realization that their futile struggles have become painfully obvious. Keros swallows his embarrassment and speaks.

"My King, sir... I mean, Your majesty, sir. I ask forgiveness. I now know what I shoulda been doing years ago. What we shoulda been doing. It would be my honor to serve in your army."

He lowers his head, bowing to the King and the rest of his friends follow in suit. Keros then looks up at the King Garras, his sentinels and Headmistress Shar Chrystel and bellows with passion in his voice.

"For the honor of Stromgard!"

★ **DAVID MILLER** ★

ANGELS AMONG US

<u>MALAKH</u>

I can't honestly tell you when I decided to do this. I guess the penchant was always in me. I was drawn to the Holy Scriptures, for my love of the Father and His creation, and the stories of heroism in the face of the Devil's evil schemes.

I was drawn to comic books, pretty much for the same reason. Deep down inside, I always felt a certain kind of sorrow at the sight of the suffering of others. I always felt like, somehow, it was my responsibility to stop their suffering, to ease their pain.

It's what got me interested in ministry. It's what got me into the Church, in the first place. It's what made me join the Army, even though I washed out. It's what made me volunteer, after the big hurricane hit, and people were flocking to our location from other states. And, I suppose, it's eventually what got me to don the costume and go out, looking for trouble.

I still remember the first night I decided to start my patrols. That day had been hectic. I was hosting an A-A meeting at the office, then there was the big charity cook-out, and then there was just... the day-to-day operations of the ministry itself. Not once has my faith in my Father been shaken. He's seen me through homelessness, madness, sadness, and sin. He's always been there for me, and I always figured it was only right to pay it forward. Today, however, the Man Upstairs dropped off quite a challenge on my doorstep... literally.

As I opened the door to exit the office, there before me, wounded in her abdomen, was a young woman I knew from the street. In fact, I had spent quite a few nights with this young lady, at the local diner, trying to convince her to come to the ministry for help, and let me get her off the corner. I assured her that no man could stand against the power of the Lord. I reminded her that countless other women had been where she had been, and they made it out of that life. I pleaded with her to at least let me take her to a hospital, and get her help when she was sick or injured. Time after time, she would turn down my offers, politely thank me for the meal, and walk back out into the cold darkness.

Quickly, I brought her back into my office, and called for an ambulance. She tried to protest, but her injury was too much for me to try to heal alone, in all good conscience. I may have studied survival medicine and first aid, but there was only so much I could risk. This young lady still had a future ahead of her, if she would just choose it. I couldn't risk killing her with shoddy second-rate doctoring. She and I took a ride to the hospital, and I set up a payment plan to pay for the work she needed done. After I cleared the plans with the hospital's human resources director and sat in the sterile waiting-room, cup of hospital coffee in hand, I couldn't help but wonder what might have been, if I had just been more persuasive with that young lady. The doctor discussed the tragic, horrid history of torture he'd seen in her X-rays and the scars littering her entire body. That was when I felt something inside me snap. I felt guilty, because I felt like I could have done so much more, as a minister and as her friend. I felt righteous fury at whoever had so damaged her, physically and spiritually. I felt hope leave my soul, replaced with a resolve I'd never felt so strongly before. I left the doctor with $50.00 and my card, and specific instructions to get the young lady some food, and a cab ride to the address on the card. He was to alert the police, so they would make sure she didn't leave my residence. As I watched the sun rise from the parking-lot, I decided to file for custody the next day. Tonight, I would put a stop to this madness, even if I had to do it one person at a time.

I picked up a completely white suit, white cloth suitcase, and a white mask. I got a can of spray-paint and some stencils. I spray-painted a pair of wings on the back of the coat, on the front of the vest and shirt, and on my suitcase. I spray-painted a halo on top of the hat, and on top of the suitcase. I finished it off with a cross between each pair of wings, and in the middle of each halo. In the suitcase, I stored water, several trail-mix bags, several sets of undergarments and ponchos, several hygiene-packs, and some phone-cards and transit-system tokens. It was a small start, but it was something. I also packed a bunch of pre-printed business-cards, with tiny maps on the back, so they could make their way to the offices if they were so inclined. Looking at myself in the full-length mirror, I smirked sheepishly. "This is crazy," I told myself, wondering if this really was what the Lord would have me do.

"Then again, I've never been one to follow the beaten path too closely."

I went out to the bus-stop, and patiently waited for the bus to pull up. I took the first bus going downtown that I could get. It was a long, quiet ride and several people were staring at me in disbelief. I can just imagine what they were thinking: "Who's this freak with the religious symbols on his clothing, and the mask and suitcase?" I cared. I won't lie. It was a little off-putting. Even so, I wanted to become a symbol of hope and faith to the people. I was so sure that was the way to put a stop to the crime and corruption in the city.

For several nights, I walked the downtown area, handing out what I had with me. I'd occasionally duck into a store to get more supplies, and then pop back out to hand them out again. I was surprised to see how many people were on the street... and appalled at how many had been turned away by my very own staff. I made a mental note to fire everyone after that first night, and hire a whole new crew of homeless people. I felt like a change was finally taking place, and I was at the forefront. I was so busy planning my nightly benevolence missions; I barely paid attention to anything else that was going on during the day. My new crew kept me updated on news, including news about some scary-sounding characters that, ironically enough were also named after angels. At the time, I shrugged it off. I had more important matters at hand. I was running a ministry during the day, and going out at night to offer charity to the people.

After the first week, I was already planning to cook up a bunch of food, hire a cab to take it to a park, and feed the homeless. I'd started printing up new cards, with the name "Malakh: Angel of the Lord," on them, and the symbol I was beginning to take pride in wearing. I was even considering talking to other people about the prospect of them becoming part of a team with me, ministering to the homeless during the evenings in similar outfits.

By the second week, things were running smoothly... almost routinely. I was having success with the nightly feeding of the homeless in the parks, but I had started to notice fewer and fewer coming for the feedings. I had also noticed more people turning my help away. At first, I thought it was because I wasn't getting them into places to live, which I had started working on. Then, I found out from one of the homeless men who would frequent my offices.

"Can't take any more," he said sadly.

"Why not? What's going on with all the homeless people that they're suddenly scared of a little charity?" I asked, feeling more than a little frustrated.

"It's not you," he reassured me. "You've been great, and I know me and my friends are all grateful for what you've been trying to do. It's just that... well..."

"What is it?" I asked, more softly this time, sensing that there was something he felt like he couldn't tell me too loudly.

My friend leaned close to me. "It's just that..." he murmured, so only I could hear, "You... well,

You dress like some of them superheroes out there... and, you know about the Omi gang, right?"

I nodded. I'd heard about them from my crew. The Omi gang was bad news. They were disgusting common crooks, masquerading as a security company. Officially, they were known as "Oniwabanshu, Incorporated." In reality, as my friends had revealed to me, they were all criminals, hired by some wealthy benefactor to go out and drum up business any way they could. They decided they'd start by forming a gang, called the Omi gang, named after the Japanese word for a type of demon that was physical in nature, not unlike an ogre or troll. Apparently, their first targets were homeless people, because they wanted to send a message to the people through the press, and they saw the homeless as some kind of subhuman targets they could have fun attacking at their leisure. When my friend told me the Omi gang was leaning hard on the homeless to stop accepting free help and join their crew, I was furious. "I'll see you later," I said, tossing $50.00 on the table. "Keep the change; meals on me."

I stormed out of the diner, fuming with rage. How dare these elitist thugs attack innocent people?! How dare they stop them from getting the help they needed?! How dare they exploit them, use them for targets, make their lives even worse than they already were?!

I rounded the corner... and saw six Omi members backing a

young woman into a corner. This woman had two children. I saw one of the Omi shove her little girl to the side, into the brick wall, knocking the girl out...

... And, that's when I lost it.

I grabbed the first piece of broken pallet I could find, and stepped into the alley. The echo of my footsteps caused them to spin around and stare at me. I could tell they meant business. Several of them had chains, knives, and even pistols. "Let them go," I growled, surprising even myself. "You want someone to pick on? Why not pick on someone your own size?"

"Yo, who do you think you are?!" The apparent leader asked, strutting forward with a pistol pointed at me. "You think you can take over our streets, punk?"

I cracked my neck. I wanted to hurt these thugs, badly. "I'll tell you who I am," I said in a low voice, removing my hat. "I'm the Angel of the Lord..." I removed my gloves. "He's angry at you and your gang, for how you've been oppressing His people..." I removed my mask. "I'm here to send a message..."

Before their leader could fire at me, I strode forward and knocked the pistol out of his hand. The gang stared in shock as I aimed at his skull, and swung for the fences. He went flying, and the others came out swinging. I threw the board horizontally at them, and ducked behind the dumpster, grabbing a handful of dirt. They thought they had me cornered...

I sprang out, threw the dirt in their eyes, and took the closest one out with a kick to the knees. He went down with a yelp, and the others started attacking... the wall behind me, because I dodged them just in time. I grabbed two of them by the backs of their heads, and knocked their thick skulls together. Picking up the chain from one of them, I backed the other two into a corner...

That's when I got shot.

The bullet pierced my stomach, a few inches to the left of my navel. To this day, I rejoice over the Lord's providence and my then-overweight physique. I dropped to my knees, feeling myself getting light-headed. I knew it could very well be all over for me, but I was comforted by two things: I knew my Lord would call me His good and faithful student on Judgment Day, and I knew that I was giving my life for a good cause.

I barely heard the shouts of fear and pain from the full assembly of the Omi. I barely saw the two dark figures that seemed to solidify from the shadows themselves, cleaning house on the gang of six... or, rather, five, since I had apparently dislocated the sixth one's knee, and he wasn't in a great position to fight. I heard a woman's voice call to me from an eternity away, "Don't you give up on me! Come on, stay with us!"

I can't really tell you much of what happened after that. I saw lights and eyes sunken into darkness. I heard the sounds of people screaming, accompanied by the sounds of angels singing. I do know that I smiled, faith telling me the woman and her children would be okay...

I awoke in the hospital, pain searing through my gut. The doctor came in. She was a lovely young Asian woman. "What... what happened?" I asked.

"You did something very stupid, and almost paid a heavy price for it," she replied. "If the ambulance hadn't shown up when they did, you might not have made it."

I sat bolt-upright in the bed... which was clearly not a good idea, because the pain forced me back down. "What... what about... the woman and her kids?" I asked. "Are they safe?"

The doctor cocked an eyebrow. "There wasn't any mention about a woman, or any children," she told me. "I couldn't tell you for sure."

This time, the pain was forgotten, as I sat up and grabbed the doctor's shoulder in desperation. "Please!" I begged, tears in my eyes at the thought of what might have happened to the family I almost died to save. "I've got to know! That gang... they were about to kill them all! Please, help me find out what happened to them!"

The doctor pried my fingers off her shoulder and backed away. "Relax, Mr. Williams," she said. "I can't promise anything, but I'll try to help you find out. For now, you have to rest. That bullet was almost fatal. I'm going to give you a little something to keep you calm. It might put you to sleep. Don't worry about a thing."

As she injected the fluid into my I.V., the last thing I heard the doctor say was, "... heart in the right place... stupid idea..."

Over the course of the next few days, I had a lot of studying of the Scriptures to do. I needed to know that I'd done the right thing. I knew the story of David, and how he wasn't allowed to build the Temple, because the Lord deemed him to be a bloody man. I knew the advice of Paul to Timothy and Titus, that pastors and deacons shouldn't be brawlers or strikers. I needed to know that I'd done the right thing... so, I read from Genesis to the Revelation. Time and time again, when the people were oppressed, I saw examples of the Lord permitting His people to fight back. In every example the nonbelievers inaccurately label genocide, the examples were there: the Lord was okay with violence, as long as it kept innocent people safe. Even Christ, when He saw the money-changers in the Temple courtyard, resorted to the threat of violence, by whipping them out. I was convinced that I had done the right thing. I wouldn't just go out cracking skulls, of course; but, if push came to shove and innocent lives were in the balance, I would make sure I could protect myself, and them.

As soon as I got back to the offices, I started looking into combative courses and tactical training. As a man without much in the way of personal finances, I took advantage of any and all free resources I could find.

It wasn't until another month later that I met my fellows in the fight against evil. It was a month later that we met the most evil human being to ever walk the Earth, short of Hitler and the coming Antichrist.

<u>MITSUKAI</u>

This city. This was the city my parents left Osaka for. This is where they wanted to raise their daughter. This was where they thought I'd be able to grow up without a care in the world, work hard, and achieve great things. They thought this would be a welcome change from the presence of the Yakuza, constantly breathing down the necks of the small business owners, and the rumors of North Korean spies killing Japanese citizens, and assuming their identities. This is the first place they felt welcome... and the last place they saw, before some punk blew them up with a car-bombing. The irony was it wasn't even them that he was targeting! When I got my hands on him, and finally got him to talk, he admitted he thought he'd planted the bomb on some Armenian crime-boss' car! How in the world did he even begin to justify confusing a Toyota Camry for a Mercedes?!

In a way, I'm glad my parents are gone. I'm not too sure they'd want to see what their precious little girl became. This is what I'm thinking as I stare out from under my black hooded duster, crouched on the roof of a near-by arcade, listening to the chatter on the police-scanner. What would they think if they knew their baby girl spent her nights striking the fear of God into the hearts of criminals, instead of relaxing after my day at the hospital? What would they think if they knew I was almost thirty years old, and had still yet to catch up to my brother, who had provided them with three grandchildren? What would they think if they knew I couldn't get over what happened to them?

...what would they think, if they knew how many times I'd come close to passing on to the next life?

It doesn't take long, before I spot my first case for the night. Three kids – they couldn't be any older than sixteen, – just went into a liquor store, dressed in unseasonably warm clothing. It reminds me of my first night on the job. As I rappel down the side of the arcade, into the inky blackness of the filthy alley below, I realize this is, in fact, the very spot where I began my career. As I climb to the top of the liquor store, careful to skirt the getaway vehicle and it's ever-vigilant driver, I remember the looks of terror, both in the faces of the teenage boy and his girlfriend, whose lives I saved, and in the criminal I stopped from rolling them for their cash. I continue to function, as if on automatic pilot, reveling in the nostalgia...

I wasn't even the hero I am today, back then. I had just started my job at the local hospital, working in the E.R.: a vocation I would grow to love not for the accolades, but for the sense that I was doing something that would actually make a difference in this world. I had just gotten off a particularly long shift, starting at 8 am, and ending at 2 am the next day. My heels clicked on the concrete, their hollow sound reminding me that I was, for the most part, alone in this neighborhood. Not the best part of town to walk through, but I didn't care. I'd been taking martial arts classes for a year, and I always had something handy that I could use as a weapon.

Suddenly, the peaceful silence was broken by the sounds of struggling and crying. I ran toward the sound, practically compelled to do something, even though I didn't know just what I could do. Peering around the corner, I saw a couple of teenagers being mugged. "That's it, nice and slow," said the attacker. Unfortunately, the boy had been a little nervous, and his hand jerked out of his pocket with the wallet. The mugger shot him...

... And, as if by instinct, I leapt out of nowhere, with a side-kick to the mugger's head. He fell over like a sack of potatoes, his handgun flying. Instinct taking control again, I delivered a back fist to the falling weapon, sending it flying halfway across the street. The mugger got up, but I quickly knocked him back against the wall, my strikes and kicks more than enough to keep him at bay. "CALL 9-1-1!" I shouted at the girl, tossing her my phone. That was all the mugger needed for a distraction, as he got up and grabbed a jagged piece of wood. Let's just say his weapon met thin air, my hands met his arm, and his body met a brick wall.

"YOU CRAZY BROAD!" He shouted, trying to punch and kick me off him. I grabbed the piece of wood. For what seemed like an eternity, I had the strongest urge to plunge the wood deep into his chest. I imagined the wreckage from the night my parents died, their charred bodies in the morgue, lying side by side. "Whoa, whoa, whoa!" His voice echoed in my mind. "Wait! Don't kill me, please! I... I got a mother! Come on, don't do it! Just let me go!"

I smacked the back of his head against the ground, just hard enough to knock him out. "Not a chance," I growled. I quickly turned on the boy who was lying there, barely able to breathe. "Hang on; you're not dying on me today!" I told him, administering first-aid as best I could. He was fading fast. Thankfully, the sirens sounded, and a couple men in white came to his rescue, followed by the boys in blue. "Are you willing to give us a statement?" One of the police asked.

"Maybe later," I told him. "I'm going with that kid to the hospital...

I got in through the rooftop entrance and dropped a smoke-bomb. With one of my bo-shuriken, I struck the transformer outside, knocking out power to the entire block. I could hear the panic in the voices of the would-be robbers, as they looked for a source of light... a source I was about to provide.

Sure enough, I descended with the rope, through a loose panel near the restroom. As soon as I got near the robbers, I turned on the strobe-light. One by one, with my tonfa, I knocked them out; except for the last one, whom I pinned to the floor. I saw his tattoo, and instantly recognized the symbol for the Omi gang... the same symbol that was on the hit-man's neck... the same hit-man, who had killed my parents. Face-to-face with me, staring in terror at my snow-white contacts, I made sure I gave him something to remember me by. "Send your boss a message for me, when you get bailed out," I hissed. "Mitsukai is coming for him." He nodded, quivering with fear, before I knocked him out. Through it all, especially after I'd used my can of red spray-paint to make the symbol of the Buddha's eyes on his chest, I had one thought running through my mind: this was way too easy...

Before the cops could arrive, I had them cuffed to the door with plastic ties. I'd ascended back to the roof, climbed down the building, and started walking, long before the cops even showed up. By that time, the blood-red smoke from my smoke-bombs had dissipated. I was one proud woman. That had been the only trouble tonight... so far...

I was almost home. *Almost* home. Curse this city.

I was about five and a half blocks from my apartment, when I happened to hear another noise. I cautiously peered around the corner of the building nearest me, into the alley. There stood some idiot, dressed all in white, holding a plank of wood in his hand. He had some kind of cross and wings on his back. I recognized the pattern: it was this new hero, who called himself "Malakh." I would see him handing out supplies to the homeless, occasionally buying one or more of them a meal. He had just started advertising – and, by "advertising", I mean he was handing out cards and spreading the news by word of mouth, – some kind of barbecues in the park, at least once per week. Nice guy, but if you ask me, his gimmick was pretty lame. It wasn't free food and ponchos that would make the city a better place... though, under the circumstances, I could see he was starting to get the picture. There were six Omi in the alley, and what looked like a homeless woman and her two kids. I couldn't let this go...

I scaled the building – which was higher than I'd expected, – and waited for just the right moment to strike. I had to admit, for a pacifist, he could handle himself pretty well... that is, of course, until one of the thugs pulled a .45 and shot him. Now was my chance. I dropped a smoke-bomb, and slid down the fire-escape, can of mace in hand.

I was doing just fine, taking on the remaining five – the sixth guy was down with a busted knee, – until one of them grabbed a little boy. "One more move, and the boy gets it," he warned. I surveyed my options. Realizing there weren't that many; I dropped the mace and tonfa, and put my hands up. The thug turned the barrel of his side-arm at me. For a moment, my life flashed before my eyes...

That moment quickly passed, however, as a shadowy figure dropped silently behind the thug with the hostage. Red eyes blazed behind his mask. I heard a sickening crack, and saw the thug's head sharply turn to the side. He dropped immediately. The others turned to face this new threat: one I'd been tracking for a while, a vigilante calling himself 'Nephilim'. I motioned to the mouth of the alley, and the homeless family ran for their lives, as Nephilim took on four guys at once. I dragged the idiot in white out of the alley, praying he hadn't lost too much blood. "Stay with me!" I pleaded, applying pressure.

"Don't you leave us now, man! You can't give up now!"

I tossed my cell to the mother – I lose more phones that way, – and yelled for her to call 9-1-1. Talk about déjà-vu. I had to change, and fast. Luckily, there wasn't much to change: I just had to pop out my contacts, and tie up my duster like some kind of makeshift backpack. The poor guy was fading too quickly. I hoped the paramedics would come in time.

Thankfully, they did. I heard the sirens blaring, like the sound of the cavalry riding in to the rescue. Police rushed past me, into an alley, while the paramedics were taking care of the guy in white. "I'm riding with," I told them. As we got into the ambulance, I could barely make out one of the police calling for a meat-wagon and some body-bags. I could also make out the sound of a number: five. I couldn't help but wonder if Nephilim had taken the guy with the busted kneecap, or if my earlier estimate had been off by one.

The paramedics were setting up an emergency I.V. I rolled up my sleeve, and offered my blood. "I'm O-negative," I assured them. I sat back and relaxed, the thought that I'd have to pull yet another shift to cover my tracks not sitting too well with me. At least the cafeteria had cookies and juice...

We arrived at the hospital. The guy was taken to the E.R. We operated, and just barely managed to save him. My transfusion made all the difference.

I was just about to go back home, when I decided to peek in on the poor guy. Vitals were stable, he was sleeping peacefully. He was going to be there for a while. I hoped he had good insurance.

Weeks passed, and I visited him once. Just once: long enough to get all the information from him that I needed. It wouldn't be too long, before he was cleared to go back home.

The night he got back home, I was waiting for him. He was living at his ministry's offices, apparently preferring to be near the action. I snuck in as a homeless woman, went to their restroom, and changed into my outfit. Once the coast was clear, I got to his office and hid in his closet. I know, it seems like a stalkerish thing to do, but I didn't want him knowing who I was, or what part I'd played in his little adventure, just yet.

He almost jumped out of his skin, when he saw the door creak open and my white eyes were shining out from the recesses of his closet. "Stay where you are!" He warned, grabbing a paperweight. "Who are you? Why are you here? If you're looking for money or valuables, I can help you get what you need, but I'm not a rich man!"

I couldn't help but laugh. He may have had guts to spare, but he was jumpy after his encounter with the Omi. That was a good thing... "Relax," I said soothingly, "that paperweight won't hurt me at all, anyway. I'm not here to rob you, or anything. Can I step out?"

He nodded. "Slow and easy, let me see your hands first." Smart. Very smart. Not too many people would think to make that request. I stuck my hands out, and let my body follow. "I'm a hero, like you," I started. "Well, not exactly like you, because I know what I'm doing on the streets. Look, I'm going to cut to the chase: I was the one who saved your life, when you got shot that one night, and I'm the one who can make you a better hero than you are now... if you're willing to trust me, that is."

He was clearly thinking my proposition over. "How do you expect to win my trust?" He asked. "For all I know, you just happened to hear what went down one night, a month or so ago, and decided to use that information to try to manipulate me."

"You're right, that could be the case," I admitted. "Of course, it could also be the case that we share a common enemy. You want to stop the Omi gang, right?"

"Oniwabanshu, Incorporated?" He asked, his expression softening. "Yeah, of course. I mean, they're targeting the homeless people I work with. They tried to kill a woman and her kids. From what I've heard, they're horrible. The worst part of it is, I don't know of anybody who's doing anything about it."

"Then, let me make a couple of suggestions," I said, approaching with one gloved hand outstretched. "First, get to know your teacher better; second, let's team up, and take down the Omi gang together, once and for all."

For a while, I wasn't too sure he'd be willing to work with me. After all, I looked like a criminal myself, I made a bunch of outlandish and possibly untrue claims and I had broken into his office to jump out and surprise him when he got back. That's why, when he gripped my hand and shook it, I was surprised. "You've got a deal," he said, "But only as long as it doesn't involve anything illegal, excessive violence, or anything immoral."

I could see this guy would be a challenge, but he was one I was willing to accept. "Sure, we'll work together on your terms," I said with a smile, flipping my hood down. "You can call me 'Mitsukai'. It's Japanese for 'angel'. What can I call you?"

He smiled slightly. "Malakh is fine for now. Maybe later on, we'll be on a first-name basis."

I made our first assignment finding out more about Nephilim. He was still out there, and because of his style of crime-fighting, I couldn't really tell if he was good or evil... on our side or against us...

<u>NEPHILIM</u>

I almost forgot. I pull out my Swedish flint, drop a few sparks on the trail of booze – expensive stuff, too, not the cheap stuff the Omi usually drink, – and casually walk away. The building explodes, sending huge chunks of wood and metal everywhere. Fortunately for me, I'm just far enough away, and behind just a safe enough hiding spot, to not have to worry about shrapnel. By the time the cops get here, there probably won't be enough left of the place to scoop up in a dust-pan. It's a good thing Mitsukai's been away for a while, or I might have to account for her interference. "Don't blow the place up just yet," she'd say. "We need whatever information we can get from them," she'd say. "Killing them won't solve anything," she'd say. I hate complications like that. I like the girl and all, but she's just too naïve... and, that new self-righteous jerk she's been spending all her free time with... he makes me want to puke. Neither of them is smart enough to realize that there's no such thing as justice... there's only vengeance. You can't eliminate evil; might as well put it out of everyone else's misery. That's a lesson I had to learn the hard way, long ago...

I was born to a mother who only loved one thing more than her addictions: beating the daylights out of her only surviving child. I guess my path was chosen for me, on the night I saw my little brother lying on the cold concrete floor of our basement, making what I would later come to know, all too well, as a "death-rattle." The beatings may not have been the worst psychologically, but they sure were the worst physically, and poor Tommy didn't have the common sense to know when to give in. I wanted that woman dead... and, I got what I wanted that night, when I snuck up to her room with a can of hair-spray and a lighter.

After her mysterious death – chalked up by the coroner to a combination of a spilled glass of Cognac and a lit cigarette... to this day, I think he knew what really happened, and just thought we'd been punished enough in our short lives; – I was taken into foster care, where I met Nicole Cruz and her husband, Bill. So much for a reprieve... they were running a human trafficking operation. Creeps of all ages, sizes and shapes would come over to their place, and take us into dark, windowless rooms. I remember the screaming. I remember the disheveled clothing, the wide-eyed looks of terror on the tear-stained faces of the children as they were led out in chains – some with really bad limps, – the scent of something vile in the air after they and their company parted ways. Apparently, it was all a test. Every month, we'd all be scrubbed down, dressed in decent clothing for a change, and taken to this mansion or that penthouse, and auctioned off. I remember what I thought was the best day of my life: the day our boss, a giant of a man whom we only knew as "Mr. Youkai," bought the whole lot of us for a cool 1.3 billion. The way I heard it, that con of a foster home shut down, and the people in charge ran off to Cancun. Up until about a year ago, they were living in the lap of luxury there... I paid them a visit, and they haven't been heard from since.

When we got to Mr. Youkai's place which was a huge skyscraper, he had us all assigned some really nice rooms. Seriously, these rooms were better than some of the rooms I'd seen in that section of the paper, where they talk about decorating houses. Each was set up like a little apartment. We got new wardrobes, too. Mr. Youkai was pretty specific about the boys wearing suits, and the girls wearing suits with skirts, but we were allowed to wear them casually when we weren't in his presence. His indentured servants told us what a nice man he was, and how well they were paid for their jobs. They told us he ran a company called "Oniwabanshu, Incorporated," which was a private security and intelligence agency. Then, they told us something that really excited us... we were to be split up into groups, put through some tests that were designed like games, and we'd be instructed according to our natural talents. We had no idea what we'd be taught... or, what Mr. Youkai would have us do...

Of course, our training began with rigorous games of 'tag' and 'hide and seek': games in which we were taught about escape and evasion, stealth, disguise, and infiltration. As time went on, those of us who wanted to continue with that training were eventually taken into the desert, where we learned these techniques and survival techniques... further expanding upon the skills we learned while we went camping. We were expected to play for an hour in the gym, and an hour in the sports facility. Some of us were trained as pick-pockets and thieves, playing 'school of seven bells'. Some of us were trained as thieves, robbers and burglars... or, as they called it, 'scavenger hunting'. Some of us were trained to make drugs, which involved learning math and science. Some were trained to con people, which involve literature and the arts. Some were trained to hack computers, which involved learning about technology and mechanics. Some were trained to sell, which meant learning about business. Some were trained to intimidate, threaten and enforce, which meant they received greater physical training. Some of us, like me, were trained in sabotage, espionage and assassination... we received all the training I just mentioned, and then supplemented it with training in law and medicine, strategy and tactics, history, psychology and warfare.

When we were old enough, we were told why we were really being trained. Mr. Youkai wanted an army of his own, capable of conquering any area and accomplishing any goal he set. He planned to start by taking over this city with legal and criminal activities, and then eventually expand, until Oniwabanshu Inc. and the Omi gang were spread out around the world and had become household names. I thought nothing of it, when I was sent out to kill people and destroy their property. At the time, I couldn't have cared whose parents, children, aunts and uncles, nieces and nephews, siblings, cousins, grandparents, spouses, friends, or coworkers I killed. As far as I was concerned, the only line I wouldn't cross was killing anyone under eighteen. Mr. Youkai was even considering promoting me to the position of deputy director. I felt like I'd really moved up in the world. Whenever I had an attack of conscience, I would tell myself this was for the best: after all, the more orphans there were, the more would be trained by Mr. Youkai and his team, the more would have jobs and some measure of security, the better the world would be. I was doing them all a favor. Besides, Mr. Youkai would only send me after people who deserved to be destroyed... right?

Wrong.

Mr. Youkai had made some enemies. Some were bad, some were good; some were powerful, and some were regular people he'd screwed over in his time. Three of them included some old Japanese couple, whose names I can't remember anymore, and a homeless woman who managed to make a lot of money in a particular illegal enterprise. They stood up against Mr. Youkai, when he tried to tear up a park to build a financial company, and again when he tried to tear down an orphanage to build a medical research facility, which he planned to disguise as a psychiatric treatment center for children with behavioral problems. That wasn't why he wanted them killed, though; he wanted them dead, because they figured out that he was the one behind the Omi gang. He'd convinced me that they wanted to get rid of our livelihood, that they wanted to deprive other unfortunate kids, like me, of the opportunities I had... never mind that I'd been a criminal since I was thirteen and a killer since I was sixteen. At the time, though my conscience ate away at me, I still complied. I literally owed this man my life. Surely, three more lives, taken before their time would go a long way toward repaying my debt to him.

Night after night, for a full week, I got closer and closer to them. I stalked outside their homes at night, I followed them wherever they went during the day, and I eventually learned just how to get close enough to them to kill them, without leaving a trace. The only problem was their daughter…

The little girl was probably no older than thirteen. She was just too cute to kill. Gap-toothed grin, sparkling eyes, hair cut into a short bob, she was so full of energy and wonder. I almost couldn't kill her mother and father… to this day, I wish I hadn't. She was always getting in the way, no matter which method I chose. When I decided to snipe them, she was always in the shot. When I decided to knife them, she always ran up to us, just as my finger was on the button of my switchblade. Anthrax? No way; the girl was the one who got the mail. Poison? As if that was even an option, what with them all eating the same food. No, I had to do something drastic, something that would ensure their deaths before the kid could get in the way…

…something that would ensure I didn't have to look into their eyes, when they slipped off to sleep for the last time.

The explosion rocked the whole block. I figured this was best: if they were going down, they would go down the best way I could make it happen: in a blaze of glory, with a pristine record to accompany them into whatever afterlife there might or might not be. Then, I saw the girl. She heard the explosion, and ran into the building, searching frantically for her parents. I couldn't stand to look at her. I imagined tears streaming down her face, screwed up from the pain of losing good parents like hers. I could already hear her sobs. Suddenly, I lost all the pride I might have had in my work. I wanted it to be done…

It wasn't. Mr. Youkai decided he wanted their daughter dead, too. I was about to refuse, until he dragged Yomi out by her hair and threw her at my feet.

Yomi was my girlfriend. She'd chosen her name after C.P.S. took her away from her home, and put her with the rest of us in foster care. Somehow, she was strong and gentle at the same time. She was funny, too, but few people knew it, because she was so distant: something I'd come to eventually learn was a defensive mechanism, so she wouldn't get hurt anymore. I don't know what caused her to get close to me, but if I was a religious man, I'd have thanked some kind of God every day for her. If she got hurt, I… I didn't think I could stand it. I begged and plead with Mr. Youkai to let her live. Take it out on me, force me to kill somebody else, kick me out, whatever other options were open, but let her go. I hadn't cried in years, but I could already feel the tears welling up in my eyes, as he back-handed the girl into the wall behind them. I lunged at Mr. Youkai, furious... and, he used the taser in his cane to shock me. I jumped back, against my own volition, and fell on my side. I could see him motion to a guard to take Yomi away. She was being dragged through a secret door. I was thinking about all the times we'd look up at the stars together, all the times we'd talk about our future after the Omi gang, all the times we would make out... my last thought was about what they might do to her, and the tears began to fall.

I awoke in the sub-basement, in a cage. The place smelled like urine, water trickled down the walls, and there was filth and mold everywhere... or, at least, everywhere I could see. I tried to get out, but I got shocked again for my efforts. "Please!" I begged my guard, a kid of maybe fourteen, "Tell me what happened to Yomi!"

I got no response. I had to get out. There was no way to tell time... Time! That was it!

Those of us who were in here longer were completely merciless. Those who hadn't been in here quite as long wouldn't have been as heartless as we could be. I started talking about Yomi, and what worried me about what could happen to her, hoping the kid was a recent recruit... no such luck. He stuck the prod through the cage. Then again, even if my original plan didn't work, there was no reason I couldn't modify it to fit the situation. As soon as he stuck the prod through, I grabbed it, yanked as hard as I could, and felt his body smack against the cage. He tried to pull it free, but I wouldn't let it go. He tried to shock me, but I kept the shocking end away. Finally, he let go and opened the lock on the cage. He stuck a .45 in... Stupid kid didn't realize that metal conducts electricity.

I left him in the cage, undressed, and went back up in the elevator, in his uniform. Of course, it was a size or three too small, but it was better than going up in my own rags. I found a guard more my size, knocked him out, and switched clothes with him. Now, I was ready to bust Yomi out...

I found my way into the room behind Mr. Youkai's office, but nobody was there. The door to the roof was open, and I could hear a helicopter. I hoped Yomi was alive: if she was, there would still be hope, even if I couldn't reach her in time. I ran up to the roof... just in time to see Mr. Youkai get on the chopper, with a body-bag. I ran for the chopper, aiming the prod for the propellers, ready to throw it if they took off.

The gunfire from the mounted Gatling guns caused me to drop to the surface... buying them just enough time to get away. It was then that I vowed to take down the Omi gang, Oniwabanshu, and Mr. Youkai himself...

So, here we are. I ran into the little girl from before, many years and bodies later. Every once in a while, we meet on a rooftop. I still can't bring myself to tell her it was me.

About a month ago, she ran into an alley, to save some idiot in a makeshift hero-costume and a homeless family. Eventually, I found out he was a minister, using that identity to get attention and get the people to be more charitable to the homeless, or something. After that night, Mitsukai took the minister under her wing, and started training him, just as I'd begun training her after she found out about Nephilim.

That night, I killed five, and took one injured criminal with me. Clearly, Mr. Youkai wasn't training them quite as well as he used to. He lay on the roof of the building, above the mess I'd left behind. I got right in his face, my mask and tinted goggles belying my rage, which was clear from the whispered growl I used. "One chance to redeem yourself," I warned. "I want answers. Your gang's plans your boss' progress with his strategy, Mr. Youkai's whereabouts... everything you know."

"A-and... and, if I refuse?" He asked.

I broke one of his arms. "If you comply, I'll make it quick and painless for you," I promised. "If you refuse... you'll have that to look forward to for another month, before I put you out of your misery."

Trembling with dread, he gave up all the information. I tossed him off the roof.

Malakh and Mitsukai worked well as a team. Of course, Malakh was Mitsukai's sidekick, but they treated each-other as equals. They were the ones solely responsible for the 300% drop in the crime-rate.

Their names were slowly becoming as infamous among the Omi gang as my own. I was glad: as long as the focus was on them, nobody would see me coming.

It was during one of their training sessions that I broke into Malakh's place. "When you two are done dancing and flirting, I have some information you may want..."

"Malakh, this is Nephilim," Mitsukai said, in way of an introduction. "He taught me everything I know."

"Everything except how to eliminate a problem," I finished for her. It was funny, how I couldn't look her in the eyes, even to this day.

"We don't kill, Nephilim," she insisted. "We're not criminals; we're crime-fighters. I'm still hoping you'll come around to our way of thinking."

I rolled my eyes. "Yeah, because I haven't been doing this long enough to know any better," I mumbled. "Do you want the information, or not?"

Malakh walked to his coffee-pot and poured three cups. "Sure, let's hear it. How do you take your coffee?" He asked.

"Irish," I joked, pulling out my journal and tearing out the appropriate pages...

Moments later, I was surprised they hadn't spit out the mud they were drinking. "How long... do we have?" Malakh asked, clearly disturbed by the information.

"A few days before they prepare, a month before it hits the fan," I explained.

They turned around, talking to each-other, and I took that chance to take off.

Stupid me, I forgot my journal... I have a feeling I'll have a lot of explaining to do...

YOUKAI

"So, tell us what you know."
"I know you're not fooling anybody with that schoolgirl routine."

That earned me another smack in the head with the nightstick.

I sat in a filthy, rotten-smelling warehouse. Blood caked the walls and floor, mixed with a substance I didn't want to even hazard a guess at. Muffled by distance and walls, I could hear the presence of vicious dogs, probably trained to attack anything with a pulse. I was tied to what very well may have been the least comfortable chair in existence, stripped to my T-shirt and boxers, soaking wet with my own sweat and blood. They had finally decided that electrocution wasn't getting them anywhere. I had given up trying to protect my contacts; now, I was just trying to spite my captors, for locking me away. I was getting a sick sort of pleasure from their exasperation, their need to torture me in new and more unusual ways, their anger at my reluctance to talk.

"Who are you trying to protect?" The cute schoolgirl asked, leaning over, whispering into my good ear. "Nobody's coming for you. They've all let you down. Why not give them up? I'll even let you watch as I dispose of them. That would sure teach them a lesson about protecting their allies."

I have to be honest, I was really entertaining the thought. "Fine," I murmured through my busted jaw, "I'll tell you."

The girl clapped her hands in some sick excuse for joy. She leaned in and asked, "Well? Who are your little friends?"

I smirked. "One is Juan, from the Taco Shack. One's Bertha, from the Shoe Barn. The big guy's Elliot, from the local library. You know; the one who looks a little like John Goodman?"

She kicked me in the face, with her stilettos. I can't even begin to tell you how much that hurt. "Boys, clean up this mess," she demanded, motioning for her mountain of a bodyguard to follow her...

I remember how I got all caught up in this mess. Three in the morning and I got a call. Triple homicide. Apparently, a couple of high-profile contributors to the Senator's campaign were walking back from a late movie with their son, when they were attacked by members of the Omi gang. Needless to say, there were three full body-bags when I got to the scene. I shook my head in a sad kind of disappointment. Even the most hardened criminals I'd had the dubious pleasure of knowing in my twenty-year career had a soft spot for children. Sure, there were criminals who killed kids, but the majority hated people like that, and tortured them every chance they got.

I crossed the not-too-foreboding yellow tape, to the chalk-lines. Fortunately, the rain had let up an hour before, and the ground was relatively dry. I got some information about the conditions of the bodies, and surveyed the scene. On a wall, not ten feet behind the outlines, there was graffiti: a demonic face, clearly of Japanese style, indicating the presence of the Omi gang. This tag wasn't fresh. It had been there for at least a month. I thought this would happen: some poor vagrant, probably from out of town, thought nothing of the leering demon's face, and set up a place for herself and her kids. How could she have known that the Omi gang were ruthless, mindless thugs, killing and maiming anything in their path?

Officer Waters was back on the beat. She'd missed three months, after she lost her partner during a drug-bust that went bad. She had never looked worse. I motioned for her to come over, while I studied the clues at hand. "You shouldn't be back yet," I told her.

Waters looked at me, through her big, dark glasses. "Got bills to pay," she said, voice jagged and ragged. She really should have lain off the cigarettes... or the screaming in the middle of the night, either one. "The boss won't let us do anything about this one either, will he?" She asked, kneeling beside me.

I took a sample of dirt from a scuff-mark. I ground it between my fingers and sniffed. I'd recognize the scent anywhere. "Maybe he will," I said. "Soot, from the ashes of a kiri tree. Looks like Nephilim was here again."

"Funny how, everywhere the Omi gang goes, he never seems to be too far behind," Waters responded bitterly. I know that, if I were her, I'd be wondering where Nephilim was when her partner was murdered. While I was in the midst of my reverie, she said something that I know I'd been thinking countless times before, but didn't want to consider...

"Almost like he's repaying a debt, by going after the gang he used to run with."

I had no idea how to respond to that, so I just stood and went back to my vehicle. "There's nothing we can do now, Waters," I said. "You look beat. Get a good night's rest. I'll turn the findings in to the Captain. All we can do is wait until morning."

Ever the hypocrite, I refused to take my own advice. I knew just where to go for information about what really happened. Recent reports indicated that the three vigilantes known as "Malakh", "Mitsukai", and "Nephilim" were not only involved; they were connected. After doing my own research, I found that each of these names were either Hebrew, or Japanese words, which referred to angels: one referred to a messenger, one referred to a benevolent spirit, and one referred to a fallen angel. The pieces were falling together really quickly. It seemed to me that the most likely place to find at least one, if not all three of these vigilantes, was at Malakh's headquarters. The evidence pointed me to a ministry nearby...

Millions of volts coursed through my body, provided by a team of cattle-prods. I always considered myself to be a pretty tough guy, but even I couldn't take this kind of punishment without letting out some kind of noise. As it turns out, that noise started out as a shriek, and turned into a strangled croak. The deceptively cute schoolgirl leaned down and lifted my bruised and battered chin. My eyelids fluttered at the sharp pain radiating from my lower jaw, defying their swelling. These brutes had really roughed me up. "You can end this anytime," she purred. "Just tell us what we want to know, and we'll drop you off at a hospital. Nobody has to know."

In spite of the agony I was in, I laughed. "Nobody but me, you mean," I told her. "I may be a cop, but I'm no narc. I'm not about to rat out these people, especially if it puts them in danger!"

The schoolgirl shook her head, and kicked the chair back. What followed next was a volley of kicks that felt like what I can only imagine it feels like to be hit by a Mack truck. The girl led her associate out of the room. "We'll be back in a few hours," she said, as I felt the viscous mess of saliva being spat onto me. I kept trying to tell myself it would be worth it... after all, the welfare of the many outweighs the welfare of the few...

I quickly circled the perimeter, peeking through windows, looking for clues to identity, location, and activity. Eventually, I decided to just knock on the front door. Finally, a man arrived, dressed in white. "May I help you, detective?" He asked. I was surprised that he knew I was a detective, but then I realized my badge was out, where everyone could see it. "I'd like to ask you a few questions," I replied. "May I come in?"

"Please do," the man answered, leading me to his office. As I looked around, I couldn't help but notice the prevalent angel motif. In fact, it was almost as prevalent as the Jesus motif. I started to feel like they might have been judging me. Did they know about all the women I'd been with, all the hearts I broke with the demands my job put on us? Did they watch all the time, as did their possibly real counterparts? I reasoned it had to be my own deeply-buried sense of guilt, getting to me through my imagination. Like everything else, it would have to wait until this case was closed.

"I'm sure you've heard, on the news, about the killing of that woman and her kids, right?" I asked, idly gazing at the office around me. It looked pretty spacious, sparsely furnished for the amount of room there was. I noticed a large duffel in the corner, which seemed to have been battered to a lumpy mess. I saw that the rest of the office had remained untouched, a light film of dust covering everything but the computer, T.V. and radio. "I wonder who could've done that. Some dude, dressed in white, is what the reports claimed."

"Hmm... yes, an interesting story, detective," the man replied, "But what does that have to do with me?"

"It's just such a coincidence that you have the same color of clothing, the same angel-related fetish, the same access to the lower class..." I continued. "Did you know we're after another vigilante with an angelic theme?"

There was not a hint of reaction to betray this man's involvement. "Weird," he said. "Tell me more; maybe, I can help you figure out who he is."

I pressed on. "Reports claim he congeals from the shadows. They say his face is the face of the Devil, himself. Strange, considering the Omi gang is supposed to be based on a type of Japanese demon. Anyway, the name's what really caught me: 'Nephilim'. Reminds me of the passage from Genesis 6."

"There were giants in those days, and also after that, when the sons of God took the daughters of men and went in unto them, they gave birth to the heroes of old, men of renown," the man paraphrased. "One of the first references to the Nephilim in Jewish scriptures, and the oldest in the Bible. However, I must remind you," he continued, crossing to the window to look outside, "That the qualifications for a man of God include that he cannot be a brawler or striker, and that he cannot eat both from the table of the Lord and the table of demons."

"Funny thing about that," I continued: "You're not the man in charge of this operation. I doubt you were given the right to take over for the real founder, while he's convalescing in the hospital."

On my way out, I called over my shoulder, "If you happen to run into this 'Nephilim' character, why don't you send him my way? I have a hunch that we have the same goals in mind. Card's on the desk. Thank you for your hospitality."

I left, hoping to receive a visit that night... which, of course, I did, though it was at my place of residence...

Hours later, my head was ringing from concussions, and I was fighting that soft, cottony feel in my skull that screamed for sleep. The only thing that kept me from passing out was the severe injuries that hour or two, or twenty, had accrued both in, and on my body. She returned. I could hear her heels clicking on the cold floor, but it sounded a little different. I looked over, and saw her in a completely different outfit, indeed. Black leggings gave way to a blood-and-fire kimono, a geisha paint-job on the face, and hair that would have been beautifully styled... had I not known the wretched evil that wore it as my captor and tormenter. She stood before me, stabbing the tip of a katana between two of my fingers with a loud clang. "Ready to sing yet, little birdie?" She asked, her voice suddenly clearer and more innocent, like a tiny bell.

I responded by spitting blood onto her tabi. "Tweet-tweet, you little imp..." I responded, coughing raggedly.

She hit me in the ribs with the spine of the katana; leaving not a slice on my flesh, but definitely causing some bruises that belied worse injuries beneath the skin's surface. "You're a lot dumber than

I thought," she said, her voice suddenly deep and raspy. Her face cold and hard, she turned away and walked out. "Leave him, Omi," she called: "We can still use him as a hostage…"

The sound of a soft cough roused me from sleep. Instinctively, I grabbed for my piece, which I kept under my pillow when I was in bed. "You've got three seconds to explain why you're-" I started, still fumbling for the missing side-arm.

"Looking for this?" A gruff, low, quiet voice asked, tossing the empty firearm on the bed at my feet. I leaned forward… and was met by a crimson face, contorted with rage, staring at me with the creepiest eyes I've ever seen. I twitched, feeling my heart race. "Okay, you must be Nephilim, right?" I asked, feeling my hands shaking from the shock's after-effect. "Tell me that's who you are."

Nephilim stood and paced in front of my bed. "You said we have a common goal. I don't think you know my goal too clearly, detective. I don't want to just bring these criminals to justice. I don't want to rehabilitate the young punks they take under their wings. They made their choices. They don't deserve a second chance, and neither did I. I'm just hoping that, eventually, I'll earn a second chance… and, I plan to do that by eliminating the Omi gang, Oniwabanshu Incorporated, and Youkai."

"Hang on!" I finally said, as Nephilim stood by the window. "Don't go yet! Let me make some coffee. You probably have a lot to get off your chest, and it's not like I could arrest you right now; I'm off-duty."

A few hours later, and the sun was rising. We had exchanged information and I tried, in vain, to stop Nephilim from pursuing his vigilante mission. I took our empty mugs to the sink. "Shouldn't you be-," I started, when I heard a slight click. He had escaped; whether through the now-closed window, or the front door, I couldn't be certain yet, but I knew he escaped my apartment. I shook my head.

One slip-up… one day, when I decided to throw back a few with the guys… one beautiful girl, who offered me a ride back to my place… and, this is where we ended up: myself on the floor, looking like I just popped out of a wheat-thresher; she and her gang, upstairs in an office, presumably discussing their plans, and my life hanging by a tenuous thread of barely-held consciousness…

I heard footsteps behind me, but I couldn't even turn my head without feeling a stabbing sensation in my neck. A soft voice whispered, "Don't worry; we'll have you out in no time. Just keep quiet." At first, I thought it was Youkai again, back to torture me herself; then, I remembered that I hadn't seen her leave the office in an hour. "What's... going on?" I asked. She quickly freed me from my restraints. "Don't be afraid," she replied. "I'm Mitsukai. Malakh is outside, patched into the security cameras, playing our eyes and ears. We need to get you out of here, before Nephilim decides to make his move. Can you walk?"

"No..." I rasped. "Barely... breathe..." She nodded understandingly, and tapped the side of her face. "Malakh, we need you in here. We've got wounded inside. He can't walk, and I'm afraid I can't just drag him out."

In a few moments, a man in white seemed to float down from the window above. Maybe it was my injuries – I was, after all, seeing spots, – or maybe I was seeing an actual angel descending from the heavens. Soon, the man in white strode toward me, and laid his trench coat on the floor. I was carefully slid onto it, and Mitsukai and the man in white led me to a near-by door. Mitsukai worked quickly on the lock, picking it open, and then we were outside. I was put into the back of a white van, and I heard the two heroes talking about whether the man in white should stay or go. After a short, quiet argument, some equipment was unloaded from the van, and I was on my way to the hospital.

I was fading in and out. Thankfully, none of my injuries were life-threatening; I'd just have to spend a few months in several casts, and a couple more months in physical therapy. As dawn broke, I noticed my only visitor was the Captain. "At least you care," I said.

"The others would've come too, but they're all on call. Apparently, after you were kidnapped, the Omi gang went absolutely bug-nuts. Robbing, murder, assault, vandalism, arson... you wouldn't believe how bad it's gotten out there. It's like a war-zone! We've even had to call on Oniwabanshu, Inc., to help us with the lack of manpower and firepower, but they can only do so much. We may need to call on the National Guard."

I called the Captain closer. "Listen closely," I murmured. "I have a lot to say. I learned a lot about what's going on. Oniwabanshu can't be trusted..."

Hours later, the Captain left my room. It looked like it was just six of us, and an entire population of vagrants, against the worst criminal organization since the Yakuza...

★ EDWARD J. STINSON JR. ★

POWER OF CHARISMA

A troubled history coupled with shortness of breath and very little time to reflect, illustrates a comedian's blundered joke, along with a show soon to fail. How can one find amusement with the body of a best friend imprinting a puddle of blood running free from a single sniper's bullet hole tunneled from his left ear to the base of the front of his neck? Three hostages sit crouched in back whimpering like abandoned puppies in fear. Their mouths are poorly gagged. The cords binding their hands are pulled tightly, numbing their limbs. The look in their eyes emulates the same feeling, as this challenge to reality acts as the cords binding their thoughts.

"Cal! Cal! The goddamn cops are comin' around the back of the house, man!! We gonna fucking die! We gonna die, man!" Cries a frantic voice bouncing from the kitchen walls, its source kneeled in the corner hugging his half-empty hunting rifle.

Rufio is Cal's best friend, Dale was also, but now he is based in his own blood dead in the living room, guilty for searching out of a window with his father's shotgun held tight in his hand. The shotgun is lying beside his corpse.

"I got it, Rufio! Calm down, I – I'm gonna fix this!" Promises Cal, snaking across the living room floor towards the three hostages.

He ignores the blare of the police horns and pulls himself to a sitting position beside the father of his ex-girlfriend. She is bound next to her mother soaked in sweat and confusion. Shaking like a leaf from the excitement and distress, Cal raises his hand towards the father after untying him and offers him his fully loaded revolver. The father slings his face over to his wife and daughter, then back to the skinny teenager's offering, stopping only to look into his eyes.

Cal cracks a small smile and instantly a shimmer of bright green energy illuminates his face and dispels with the speed of a single eye-blink. The father clutches the revolver, gets up and moves toward the back of the house passing the staircase for safety.

Cal uses the opportunity to address his ex-girlfriend by removing her gag, "Dale's dead Barbara, and i-it's your fault! You heard me! It's your fault!" He pushes past her mother and leans his face against her cheek. "He was one-a-my best friends, you whore! Now, he's dead for fucking around with you."

A barrage of gunfire can be heard from the back of the house as the stutter of automatic weapons respond in kind. A heavy tumble across the floor finds completion with a deep thud as the gunfire ceases and assumption cries out.

"DADDY!!!" Screams Barbara, as her mother shrieks against her gag in the like. Cal looks into the eyes of both Barbara and her mother smiling as he releases the familiar shimmer of green energy that has made him a controlling bully for the last few years of his young teenage life. The duo slide back into false relaxation and become eerily calm.

"Shit! Cal, these fuckers are moving up! They're gonna try to bust in on us! Cal, we gotta do somethin'!" shouts Rufio from the kitchen, before cracking off two rounds from his hunting rifle.

Amazingly, no gunfire is returned.

A lone deep cough from a weapon across a local police officer's hood delivers a blistering canister of tear gas into the kitchen window next to Rufio. Falling back onto a trashcan, he scrambles around the tiled floor and tosses his jean jacket onto the spinning canister while puking on a dining room chair. The jacket bursts into flames, igniting a small corner of the kitchen.

Cal glimpses the commotion and calls out to his friend, "Rufio! What's happening?" His reply is a feeble dash from Rufio into the living room, resulting in a hasty escape through the front door and into the arms of a waiting SWAT team.

Cal pulls a shirt across his face, abandons his hostages and escapes deeper into the house up the staircase. He stops short of the top floor as the darkness before him emits an uncanny feeling. He moves nothing, save his head, which slowly turns just enough to see that no policemen have barged through the doors of the living room. It beckons the question of, 'Why?', unless this entire action was planned. The plumes of tear gas that spread along the walls and floors engulfed all that was intended and dissipated. It was weaker than normal... that is, unless this entire action was planned. The hostages begin to regain their senses as the police lights outside flicker intensely through the windows. For this young comedian the amusement from his haphazard actions was dying quickly. He had no applause coming. His conscience urges him not to go back down the stairs, as what became an act of gratification through revenge, turned into something beyond sinister. For Cal, losing control was his anxiety and now he could not go back the way he came. It is the cold, deep fear within him that recognizes the presence within the gloom ahead, which is the only true path that he can take.

A shift in the dark dusk preludes the dank silhouette stepping towards this arrogant teenaged kidnapper. The few paces heard are less than sound and more than warning. Cal squints his eyes at the figure hoping for clarity through obscurity, only to find someone or something that he has never seen before. Facing him, a lurid warrior stands. The warrior peers into the youth's soul without eyes that can be seen - he becomes the answer to the question of fear. His mask, with a V-shaped visor of non-reflecting, indigo glass, obscures his eyes but not the intensity of his stare. His body is chiseled and tight. He is the predator, anxious before the capture of his prey. His intent is focused through his shaded uniform, defined by the tenacious symbol of a hawk on his chest. He holds no weapons and he makes no move.

Stunned by this sight, Cal seeks to take control by removing the shirt from his face and staring into the visor of the warrior who blocks his escape. Cal smiles slowly, locking in the final component that activates his extrability to mentally control others. The warrior's indigo visor melds into a cryptic deep black almost instantly, reacting from Cal's attempt. The warrior reaches out his hand clutching the throat of his target. The teenager grasps the forearm of his assailant hoping to pry it loose. He lifts Cal from the ground while drawing his free hand back into a battle-hardened mighty fist.

He slams his fist into Cal's cheekbone shattering it and breaking his jaw. The impact yanks the youth's body sideways and forward in an attempt to pass the shock through it. His thighs tighten and his fingers dig into the uniform of the dark warrior. The hawk-wearer reels back again as tears from Cal find way over collapsed flesh to gather around his clutch.

Blood seeps from his ear as voice trembles through a shattered jaw to beg for the selfish life that he holds so dear. "P-Puh-weeze…

Puhweeze, d-don't kw-kwill me..."

The warrior shifts his clutch ever-so-slightly and slams his fist directly into the front of Cal's face. His nose crunches downward from the pressure, as the bridge of it cracks allowing the release of multiple teeth staggered in placement and trailed by blood. The youth's hands drop from his holder's and dangle to his side as his thighs release tension and both of his legs follow suit. With a motion very similar to that of one discarding trash, the warrior flings the kidnapper down the stairs, ensuring that his body receives treatment much like that of his face.

The police enter the living room led by a single FBI agent who walks over to inspect the teenager before the medics begin their process to stabilize him. The agent moves to the top of the stairs to address the warrior.

"Good job, Ghosthawk. He needed eye contact and a smile in order to use his powers. We're categorizing it as 'Charisma'." He looks over his shoulder back towards the youth, "That disfigurement you gave him looks like it's going to be permanent. Heh, problem solved huh?"

The Ghosthawk steps back into the embrace of the shadows.

"By the way, thanks for saving the girl's father earlier by tackling him to the ground. Tonight we only lost one life. It could have been much worse. "

The Ghosthawk leaves after an elusive nod and heads off to his next mission.

> **EXTRABILITY** - *Possession of abilities greater than that of the normal man.*
>
> *- ELITE FORCES DIVISION*

✮ QUINTIN BAKER ✮

THE SHADOW HUNTER

Night had fallen in Haven. The city, while beautiful during the day seems even more so at night. A strong ocean breeze blew in from the east making the summer night unseasonably cool and inviting for many of the people living here. The streets downtown were especially bright and busy with activity. People walked on crowded sidewalks as cars cruised down double lane highways enjoying the pleasant night. Neon lights and techno music could be heard from nearly every avenue as bar owners and nightclub promoters lobbied for all the potential patrons. Amiris stood atop one of the taller buildings in the area and took it all in. He looked off into the distance at the huge, gray stone walls that wrapped around the city like great protective arms, shielding it from the perils that lurked outside.

"Too bad those walls don't keep all the danger away." He lamented to himself.

Amiris slowly brought his vision back to this small part of town. He peered down from his high perch into the near black alleyway below. There was a light at the front of the small side street but its primary function was to provide light to the main sidewalk, leaving most of the alley way dark. He could see keenly in the dark though, evil was lurking there. Amiris shook his head in disgust.

A cry from the main street drew his attention from the alley. He saw two women; one of them a police officer, were chasing a young man down the sidewalk. The officer was tall and fair skinned. Her thin body moved gracefully through the crowds of people, as her bone straight, blonde hair whipped around her. She wore a very form fitting, dark blue uniform that made her look even thinner. The woman next to her was, in stark contrast much more curvaceous. She wore a black and gray, spaghetti strapped top. It was cut low at the collar, displaying her supple breasts quite clearly. She also wore tight, white shorts, which barely made it to her thighs. Her skin was the color of almonds. She had shoulder length curly brown hair, which ended in caramel tips. She was obviously dressed to get attention, and it looked like she had gotten some.

The mugger; a teen by his appearance, wore simple blue jeans, and white tee shirt. Looking closer Amiris saw that the kid clutched something gray underneath one of his arms. He frantically pushed through the busy sidewalk with the other, desperate to escape the two women behind him. The women moved after him with equal conviction; slipping around, and through the bystanders. The cop was shouting repeatedly for the boy to stop, but it was obvious to all that he had no intensions of complying. Amiris watched, with a smirk as the thief turned into the dark alley below him.

When the two women reached the entrance to the alley the officer called for the man to come out. No one answered. Straining to see into the darkness, the police woman could barely make out the interior. She saw a large dumpster to her left. To her right were several trash cans and trash bags. Drawing her gun and a flashlight the cop slowly started to make her way into the alley. Still in the light the officer was stopped by the other woman.

"You can't go in there alone, it's too dangerous." She said in a whisper.

"I have to." The cop replied. "I can't tell if there is a way out through the back or not and if there is he could be getting away."

"Can you call for back up?" The woman retorted.

"If I was sure this was a dead end I would, but it would take too long to wait." The cop said taking a step into the alley.

"Well, I'll come with you." The woman stated. "It is my bag after all."

The officer nodded in reluctant approval. "Ok, just make sure you stay close behind me." The officer ordered. "I don't want you getting hurt in there."

The woman nodded and placed her hand on the police woman's shoulder as they made their way in to the alley. Focusing their attention on the alley itself the activity from the main street faded away. The nauseating smell of urine and garbage mingled to assault the women's senses. Shuffling vermin could be heard near the trash cans and dumpster. With every step they moved further and further into the darkness. The longer they were inside it the more it seemed like the alley itself was alive. Dark and menacing, dank and dingy, it felt as if it were dripping with unseen dangers.

They crept deliberately down the left side of the alley along the side of the dumpster. Keeping the dumpster at her back allowed the officer to scan the right side of the backstreet easily. When they had gotten to the edge of the dumpster the cop was fairly certain the mugger was hiding around the corner. She steadied her nerves, and jumped out from behind her cover. There was a man there. Shocked by her sudden appearance the man reached out to push her away. Fear and surprise took her steadiness. Her trigger finger recoiled, and the gun went off. The bullet hit the man square in the chest. He fell back and collapsed against the wall. The police woman's eyes widened in horror. The man she shot was not the purse snatcher.

Stepping back in disbelief, the cop nearly tripped over the woman behind her. In a near panic the officer moved her flashlight around the back of the alley. She saw the mugger crouched along the back wall of the side street.

"I saw what you did." He said, smiling. "That wasn't nice Mrs. Officer. You killed him. I saw it." His voice as high pitched, almost adolescent.

"Shut up!" The officer demanded.

"What are we going to do?" The woman said from behind the cop. Her voice filled with dread.

"I don't know." The officer replied. "I don't know."

"I have an idea." The voice came from the darkness to the officer's left.

Quickly turning the flashlight and gun in the direction of the voice, she saw that the words had come from the man she shot. He was standing up, brushing the alley filth off of his clothes. She wondered how this was possible. She had shot him, squarely by her recollection. He should be dead or at least dying. Still pointing her gun she backed away from the man.

"Since you thought it was OK to kill me, how about I kill you." He said, smiling at her. His smirk revealed long white fangs.

"A vampire" The cop mouthed to herself. "Run lady, run!" She yelled, glancing quickly over her shoulder. Her voice was filled with urgency. She turned quickly back to the vampire. Her gun was trained on the creature's chest but she had already shot him once and she had no idea if the threat of being shot again would keep the blood sucker at bay.

"Why should I run?" The woman whispered coolly into the officer's ear. The woman's words; filled with such an eerie sense of satisfaction sent a cold chill down the cop's spine. "I thought it was a great idea." She continued, and now the officer could hear the woman's smile in her voice. Before the police woman could react the woman grabbed her by the wrists and forced them to her side. So forceful was the woman's grip that the cop dropped her gun and flashlight.

The purse thief strode calmly up to the vampire and put his hand on the monster's shoulder. "That was an awesome plan Ant." He said with a laugh. "I haven't had so much fun hunting in decades." He continued.

"That reminds me," the vampire started, pointing a finger at the mugger. "Here we are, all set to turn this woman into a dry husk of a corpse and we haven't even introduced ourselves. Where are my manners?" He continued, feigning embarrassment. "My name is Anthony but my friends call me Ant. My associate here is Damien, and you've met Patricia." He said, gesturing towards the woman holding her from behind. "And you are Officer Kelly Davis." He noted, looking at her name tag. "Well Officer Davis, it is going to be our pleasure to have you for dinner.

Anthony and Damien approached Officer Davis slowly, baring their fangs hungrily.

"We all know it's illegal for vampires to hunt humans in the city." Davis cried, desperate for a reprieve. "When the High Lord finds out about this he will hunt you down, and execute all of you in public. He's not going to have his authority challenged you know this. If you let me go I won't say anything, I swear. No one will know and we all get to go on living, or whatever it is you do." Despair could be heard clearly in the woman's voice.

"That's a fine offer Ms. Davis" Anthony replied smoothly. "But I'm going to have to decline. You see I'm the High Lord's chief lieutenant. So he is never going to find out about this. And, if by some chance he does find out vampires are hunting in the city, well, the trail will lead him to some other poor vampire. I'll make sure of that."

Davis' mouth hung open. "You're Chief Lieutenant Anthony Dumar?" She asked, shocked by the revelation. "This doesn't make any sense. Why are you breaking the laws you helped make?"

"Because my dear," he said holding her chin in his hand. "I feel like it." The words came out slowly, resonating with such cold malevolence that it caused the blood to drain from Davis' face. "Now, enough with the questions. I'm starving, and your neck looks so inviting."

Anthony was just about to sink his fangs into the officer when an unfamiliar voice startled him and his companions. "This has gone far enough. Let the girl go." The voice came from the back of the alley. It was clear and powerful with a distinct authority behind it. They all looked back, eyes wide with surprise. Davis strained to see who was there, but she did not have the keen night vision of the vampires. The others could see Amiris perfectly though.

He was taller than any of the blood suckers, easily over six feet. A smooth mahogany complexion graced his youthful facial features. His hair was cut neatly low with thin sideburns connecting to a thin goatee. The young man was dressed in all black. The shirt; long sleeved and fitted, was padded in some places and reinforced in others. He wore loose fitting cargo pants; the bottom of each leg was tucked neatly into his boots. The boots themselves were tied tightly around Amiris' shin. The metallic toe of the boots caught the vampire's attention as it glinted subtly in the darkness. But it was the man's weapons that truly unnerved the monsters. A dagger was holstered on his hip as well as a sword on his back. Amiris looked ready for a fight.

For a few quick seconds Anthony looked at Amiris perplexed. In truth Ant didn't know what it was he was looking at. His mind was nearly overwhelmed with thought. Was this a human? What kind of human would want to sneak up on a group of vampires, and furthermore, what kind of human could, even if he did want to? They should have smelled him coming, heard his footsteps, something. Even now he gave off no scent, not even a heartbeat. Anthony was sure this wasn't a vampire either. Even vampires gave off a scent; they could also feel each other's presence through the undead aura all vampires gave off. It was almost as if the man they were looking at, and heard speak was not really there at all.

"Who the hell are you?" Anthony said, more demanding than asking.

"Knowing who I am is not a prerequisite to doing what I say." Amiris replied "Now, release her and don't ever let me catch you hunting humans again. Now go."

Amiris' words; dripping with the purest condescension enraged Anthony. He grabbed Officer Davis from Patricia and threw her violently into the trash dumpster. The woman collapsed on the ground in a heap and did not move.

"There, she's free." Ant said through clinched teeth. "Now you're going to take her place." The vampire lieutenant walked deliberately towards the impertinent young man. As he walked his fingers elongated and his nails grew into long, boney claws, as did the other two vampires that were following him. He bore his fangs in a threatening grimace, a promise of pain written clearly on his face.

Sword and dagger leaped from their sheaths in a flash as Amiris prepared for the vampires attack. "Since you crave true death so badly blood sucker, I will oblige you." He replied. With his sword in his right hand and the dagger in the left, Amiris settled into a defensive position.

The vampires spread out the width of the alley and charged Amiris together in an attempt to surround him. Their attack was savage; fangs snapped, and claws slashed at inhuman speeds. But as fast as the undead monsters were, Amiris was faster; his hands moved in a blur deflecting and parrying every vampyric strike. His deft footwork kept him in perfect balance as he spun in tight circles, meeting every threat. Time and again the vampires struck at perceived openings only to be denied by a sword or dagger.

Not being able to land a hit on this young foe was only half of the undead group's problem. With every deflection and parry, searing stings were sent coursing through the vampires. It was quickly apparent to them all that this man was using silvered weapons; and any contact with it would weaken even the strongest vampire. Anthony, being older and better versed in combat saw the brilliance of the strategy. Every time one of those silvered weapons touched a vampire it weakened the monster just a little, but with as many attacks as the three of them were making all the man had to do was parry and it would not be long before they were too weak to fight at all; and then it would be the end of them. Anthony realized it then, it was all a ploy; this, whatever he was had pushed his buttons hoping to draw them into a wild fight. The vampire lieutenant had to admit this man was cleaver. He also had to admit that this fight had clearly become more than he bargained for. He had to rethink how he was going to deal with this thing in front of him. "Damien, Patricia, fall back. This isn't working." He said, quickly moving from the young man.

Staying in his defensive stance Amiris eyed the vampires around him suspiciously. They had finally figured out what his plan was, but he knew that silver would drain a vampire's strength until it was on the brink of death, simply from its touch. He also knew he had tapped each of them many times during his parrying. There was no way to gauge just how much power he had stripped from them, but he saw that of the three of them, only the one giving orders had no obvious signs of fatigue. The other two were breathing heavily, hunched over and their open wounds did not regenerate the way that vampires normally do. "It doesn't look like your subordinates are going to be able to play much longer." Amiris said to Anthony, lowering his weapons and taking a more relaxed posture.

"You should worry more about me and less about my underlings." Anthony replied, hatred clear in his voice.

"Oh you are going to get my full, undivided attention very soon," Amiris retorted "but I want you to really see what you chose to fight." Then he gave Anthony such a wry grin that the hairs on the back of the vampire's neck stood up.

Still smiling, he turned to look at Damien. The vampire caste a baleful look that turned to shock as Amiris disappeared. Damien's eyes nearly bulged out of their sockets. He looked at Anthony whose gap mouth expression gave him no help. He then turned to Patricia who was similarly bewildered. His next idea was to scan the alley itself to see where the guy had gone. He took several steps around the alley when suddenly his back arched back greatly with a violent spasm and his chest exploded open. Amiris reappeared behind Damien; his sword hilt deep in the vampires back. Only the clothing remained as Damien's body turned into a pile of dust on the dirty ally floor.

Seeing the way her friend died in front of her, stole Patricia's will to fight. She began backing quickly out of the alley. She wanted to turn and run full speed out of the place, but did not want to let that thing out of her sight. It did not matter though, just as with Damien, Amiris vanished right before her eyes. She stopped cold. Her eyes darted back and forth nervously, searching for any sign of the man. "Where are you?" She mouthed to herself, her voice just barely audible.

"Right behind you." Amiris whispered into her ear.

She wanted to scream. She wanted to be away from this horrible place. But all she could do was jolt as the silver dagger slipped through her black heart.

"Ashes to ashes, and dust to dust." Amiris said to the female vampire as her body became little more than another pile of filth in the alley.

Anthony watched it all in horror. This, thing had killed two of his dearest friends, easily by the looks of it. He had never seen a vampire rendered so completely helpless in all his long years of life. He knew he would be next; he was stronger than the others but not strong enough to defeat this monster. He turned and ran towards the alley opening. He turned and moved with that inhuman vampire speed, but only made it a couple of steps. In the middle of his run he fell, or rather he was tripped. Hitting the ground hard he looked to see what he could have tripped over. It was the outstretched leg of Officer Davis. She grinned at him as their eyes met, and he returned it with a look filled with so much hatred that it washed away the officer's smile, and drained the blood from her face. He moved towards her, his fangs were bared and one thought was in his mind; if he was going to die he would make sure this woman went to her death first.

Anthony's arm was cocked to rend the woman savagely but a silvered sword appeared at his throat, halting the death blow.

"You should worry more about me and less about the human in the alley." Amiris said, moving to stand in between the vampire and the human.

Fueled by unadulterated hatred, Anthony lashed out at Amiris, renewing the ferocious attack he had used earlier. Once again the sword and dagger were up meeting every one of the vampire's blows. Anthony ignored the burning pains from the silver. He would accept a thousand strikes from them in return for one clean slash. They fought for what seemed like a lifetime for Ant. He felt his strength waning, the opening he hoped for was not going to come. He knew in his black heart he was going to die here, but he would not go down easily. In a final act of desperation he grabbed both sword and dagger with his bare hands. The pain was almost unbearable. Anthony screamed to the heavens, and then lunged at Amiris; his fangs were ready to tear into the man's throat.

The undead jaws snapped shut tight. But his attack did no damage. The deadly fangs had passed harmlessly through the young man, as he became completely intangible. The swords too lost their tangibility. With nothing solid to brace his forward momentum against, the vampire was pitched totally off balance, stumbling right through Amiris and down to the ground.

"What are you?" Anthony roared at Amiris in outrage, as he stumbled to his feet to stand before his foe.

"Your executioner." Amiris replied coldly. And with a sudden slash from his glimmering silver sword Amiris cleanly sliced Anthony's head off of his body.

Amiris did not pause to watch the vampire turn to dust. Instead he headed directly to the injured police woman. She was sitting on the ground leaning against the dumpster. She did not seem to have any serious outer wounds but Amiris was sure she had a concussion. He sheathed his weapons, and offered her a hand. She took it and he pulled her up to her feet.

"Are you OK?" He asked, checking to make sure she did not have any bite or claw marks.

"Other than a few bruises, and a mammoth headache I'm fine." She replied as she ran her fingers through her hair. "By the way, thanks for saving me. I don't really know how to repay you, but if you ever need anything, just ask me, and you got it."

Amiris smiled, and then turned to walk back towards the end of the alley.

"Wait," Davis called from behind him. "Who are you?"

"My name is Amiris." He replied without turning around.

"OK, Amiris," she pressed, with a sigh. "What are you?"

Amiris stopped walking then. He stood silent for a long moment then made his way back to the police officer. "I am a Wraithling." He said, looking at her intensely. We are a race of beings that live in the veil that separates the living from the dead. Long ago we learned how to move between our plane and yours. You would be surprised at how many of my people are actually on this plane."

"So there are more like you out there?" Davis asked, and her eyes were wide with wonder.

"Yes." He said, turning away once again. "But don't expect them to help you at all. Most of my people believe that we should only be spectators in your world. They come here only to watch the evil, as it slowly envelopes this plane. As far as what actually happens to the people here; they don't care.

"So why do you?" She asked softly.

Again Amiris was silent for a long moment. "It's because there are few creatures anywhere that can outmatch a vampire; we can. I believe it is our responsibility to fight for those who can't. It shouldn't matter what plane you live on, those who are strong must protect those who are weak." Once again he began walking to the back of the alley. So I'll fight for you. From the shadows I'll help you push back the evil. I do it for the simple fact that it is the right thing to do."

After another long moment of silence, Davis called to Amiris. There was no response. She flashed her light towards the back of the alley but saw no trace of him. Turning the flashlight to the three piles of dust that had been vampires only a few minutes before, she smiled, and turned to walk out of the alley way. The city had a hero, she thought; a hunter in the shadows. And if he was serious about what he said, then things in Haven were about to get very interesting.

★ **ADELEYE YUSSUF** ★

WEAPONXMITH

Lying on my bed face up, I stared at the static ceiling fan. The noise of people yelling and the sounds of gunshots coming from the street below filling my ears. Our apartment was on the third floor of the building. It was late and I was getting ready to sleep, but the noise was so loud that I had lain down on the bed for half an hour without dozing. I didn't bother to check the noise coming from the street because it's a common thing. I could think of a thousand things that may be happening down there and none of them would interest me. Either some gangsters are doing their chase 'em and shoot 'em thing or some monster had broken into the city or cops were chasing another drug dealer. Things we face in Vegran city every day.

There was a knock on my bedroom door. I got up reluctantly, still in my pajamas, the bed creaking loudly. I put on my slippers, walked to the door and slightly pulled it open. My dad stood there. He beckoned at me to come with him. He was putting on his lab coat and I was sure this was about some experiment or newly built weapon because that is what he does.

I followed him into the lab, his really messy lab. His movement was too slow for a man at fifty-two. I noticed that he was not wearing one of his "hey son, come checkout this cool stuff I made" expressions. He was somber, so I kept my silence. He asked me to lie down on the lab bed. I took off my shirt because I knew how it's done. I lay down gently and he strapped me to the bed. He had never experimented on me before, so I was surprised.

His laboratory is a really small one but has invented more than any other in the city; weapons, machines, armors - and a lot of them. Dads' creations hang on its walls, machines that some have never set their eyes on, not even me. I'm always his first consultant whenever he tries to make anything new. Which, as far as I know, none of them had ever been able to meet his expectations. He had spent half of his entire lifetime trying to stop corruption and crime in this city. He joined the Vegran City Police Department. He had been an armor maker before he met my mother. His occupational hazard was what actually led to her death. She died two years ago, murdered by Gordon, the city's worst nightmare.

Gordon was an ex-convict who had vowed to send the city to its doom for imprisoning him for nine years. He wasn't just an ex-con; he was a big time drug dealer. He committed murder several times, raped, robbed... hell, he deserved to go to prison. But he didn't seem to think so. He has lot of people working for him, some scientists building him machines; he even had Moles in the VCPD. He had also tried to set loose a bunch of killer-robots in the city but thanks to dad's ultra-X95, he failed. Ultra- X95 was one robot known to be the hero of the city some time ago, but it was now destroyed. Dad had used his advanced robotics skill to save the city from Gordon uncountable times.

"I'll need you to hang on tightly, Mark," he said as he operated his machines.

"The strap is tight enough."

"You are my only hope now; this will all be over soon."

Then I knew there was a problem. He returned to me and stroked my hair, crying helplessly. I didn't know what to say. I wanted to say something, I knew I had to say something, but I was speechless. I didn't know what to expect. Thoughts rushing through my brain: Is this a deadly experiment? Is it too dangerous? Will I survive it? Damn it, why is he crying? He should have told me about this earlier. I was in the dark, and the slightest ray of light was hard to find.

"You are the city's only hope." Then I noticed he was now holding my hand. The grip got tighter and I couldn't stop the tears from streaming out of my own eyes. He turned back to operate his machine, and then there was a countdown from a female computer voice.

"Cybernetic implant commencing in twenty seconds."

He plugged a cable under the bed on which I was strapped. I felt a strong shock running down my spine. The countdown continued. Dad took a seat beside my bed, careful not to touch it or me.

"You are the best thing that ever happened to me son," he started. "When I met your mother, I was so blindly in love and when I lost her, I thought that love and happiness was gone forever. As you grew up, I knew you were a replacement. You brought my happiness back, you have always been a good boy Mark, the best I can ever wish for, and you've always made me proud. I want you to know that I love you son, and I always will."

"Cybernetic implant commencing in fifteen seconds."

I started to feel like I was being electrocuted, my eyes bulged and I started to scream in agony, my body arching off of the bed, it was a nightmare.

Suddenly, more gunfire filled the air, but this time it was close, nearby, like right outside our apartment. There was a bang on the door, really hard, several more followed and there came a crashing sound as the door splintered inward. Dad had locked the door of the laboratory when we came in. The apartment was invaded, and I had a feeling it was Gordon. Strapped to the bed, the agony continued. It felt like my veins were trying to erupt through my flesh. I roared loudly, loud enough to alert the invaders; they came beating the laboratory door. Dad was sobbing really bitterly now.

"Cybernetic implant commencing in five seconds"

Electric sparks were dancing around visibly on the outer part of my body and my vision was fading. I couldn't control any part of my body, it had been taken over by whatever Dad was doing. I noticed that my vision wasn't the only part of me that was fading, everything was.

Before my soul was finally gone, I heard Dad's voice which sounded like a whisper, though he must have had to scream aloud for me to hear him across the distance between my soul and the world around.

"Good luck son."

As I lost my soul to the implant, Dad's final statement was followed by a loud crash. It could only mean one thing.

I was stunned by the sight of the all-white environment above me as I lay motionless on the bed which was white as well. Easing into light from the darkness of my closed eyes I was first confronted by the sight of the extremely neat white ceiling ahead. The ceiling in my bedroom hadn't been cleaned or painted in years and it's hard to remember what color it was, but I was damn sure it wasn't white. Hanging from the ceiling was a shiny white ceiling fan, spinning swiftly. Even the walls were white. I bolted upright into a sitting position ready to panic. I tried to relax, convincing myself that I was in a dream. As I took several deep breaths, the sound of the opening door captured my attention. A nice looking female came into the room. She was carrying a tray with both hands, filled with stuff I couldn't see from where I sat. She was dressed in a white dress, with four pockets, that stopped above her knees. She wore a white nurses' cap over her blonde hair. She closed the door behind her as she came in.

"Where the hell am I?" I screamed at her, startling her badly. She yanked the door open and ran out in fear, making a really weird sound as she left. The door stood open and there was a white wall outside facing the door way. I got up as if to chase her when I felt something pulled out of my right arm. It was an IV tube. I traced it back until it led my eyes to an IV pole. I noticed there was another one on my left arm. I pulled it out in anger. I took a better look at the room and realized that I was in a hospital. I felt some sort of coldness running in my veins, and I was confused. I spun about trying to make sense of things.

Another entrance through the door distracted me again, but this time there were four people. The first one closest to me, I recognized as the doctor. He was in a lab coat which was unbuttoned, a vertically striped shirt with a blue tie, and brown trousers. Standing behind him was another nurse, a redhead, dressed the same as the first nurse. On her right was a heavily built, dark skinned guard in uniform, holding a baton on his left hand. I didn't see her at first, but a closer look identified the girl behind him as the first nurse, still carrying her tray. They all stood just inside the open door.

For a hospital ward, the room wasn't big enough for five of us. Though bigger than my own bedroom, there was only room for just one more person, and maybe a small dog. A lot of space was occupied by the gigantic medical bed, big enough for two, a white bedside cabinet, and the IV pole.

"Where am I?" I repeated my question in a more reasonable voice.

"Relax Mr. Carson," the doctor said as he moved closer to me. He placed his hand on my shoulder. "You're at the hospital and you shouldn't be stressing yourself. You're just now recovering from a massive damage to your internal organs."

"What happened to me?"

"A laboratory accident."

I started recalling what had happened at Dad's laboratory. Images flashed through my brain. I remembered the experiment, then dad, Dad! Thinking of him made my heart constrict in pain.

"Where is my father?" I asked, adding a little volume to my voice. There was a long pause and awkward expressions on the faces before me, except the guard, who I guess didn't even care.

"I'm sorry Mark" he said at last, patting my shoulder. "Dr. Carson is dead."

The last D word hit me hard; I didn't want to believe it, I couldn't believe it.

"No!" I screamed. "It's a lie, you are a bloody liar!" There was another pause. "I want go home now." I said as I made for the door way.

"I'm afraid not, Mark. I can't let you."

"Why?"

"You're not strong enough yet."

He put both hands on my chest to stop me. I grabbed his hands and effortlessly hurled him onto the sickbed. He landed hard and groaned in pain. I didn't care. I raced towards the door. Both nurses scurried out of the room, just like the blonde did, but this time they slammed the door behind them. The guard, fear creeping onto his face, hit me across the face with his baton. My head snapped sideways but the rest of my body didn't move. I felt nothing. I turned back to him. He was a bit scared but struggled not to show it, still holding his baton and willing to use it. I kicked him hard before he could, the force of the blow knocking him through the closed door, shattering it. He landed on the concrete floor of the hallway. He made no attempts to get up, but he was breathing.

I stepped out of the room, crouching to avoid the jagged edges and trying to avoid stepping on the guard. I looked back and saw the doctor still struggling to get to his feet, groaning heavily. I walked along the hallway. There were doors to the right, and each was numbered. I headed towards the door at the far end, tagged "STAIRS." I hurried towards it. The door was pushed open before I was halfway there, more guards in the same uniform rushed in, about six of them. I guess the nurses must have called, since these guards had guns and those guns were aimed at me.

"Stop right there!" One of them shouted.

I paused and raised my hands slightly. They began to move forward. I watched every step they took. With my right shoulder, I pushed the door beside me into an empty room. There was a window directly opposite the door. I went for the window as the guards charged into the room after me. The window wasn't too high and was shut. I dove through it, followed by gunfire.

The window was a shortcut to the street; I fell in a rain of shattered glass onto the top of a black SUV that was parked on the side of the street, breaking my fall. I crashed into the car and broken glass showered onto the street. People scattered in a crouching run to avoid the shower of glass, a few women and children screaming in fear. I got up quickly and looked up at the hospital. The window from which I fell was about forty feet high; two guards were standing there, pointing the guns at me. I rolled from the crushed car top to the ground. The rain of glass became a hail of gunfire turning the street into total chaos. I took cover by the car, and then raced to across the street where I sighted an alley. I cut down the narrow passage, which was filled with trash cans and bags, bypassing them as I ran to the other end of the alley where I hijacked a Ford truck and drove away.

I stared at the gray five-story building in front of me. The colors were still shiny. None of the windows were broken, still new. Looks like this building hadn't had the experience of the rough side of Vegran city. The building was standing on the land that used to be occupied by our crappy old three-story building. I came here looking for my home, but somehow it was gone. I shook my head in disbelief.

The building was built along a two-way road. The apartment balconies were close enough together that you could easily jump from one to the other.

I was sitting in the truck, which I parked opposite the building. I was wearing a red jacket that I found in it. I started the truck up again, crossed the road, and went straight to the building, my mind burning with questions.

My body was cut in several parts from shards of glass, bruised from falls and scratches, and wounded from bullets I never felt. When I was trying to put on this red jacket I found beside the driver's seat, I found these marks on my body. I was perplexed by the marks of the bullets that didn't penetrate my skin, cuts that didn't bleed, and there was a large hole in my chest; I didn't know where that came from but I knew none of the guards had carried a bazooka. There were matching smaller holes on both of my forearms. They weren't bullet holes I was sure, but I had no idea where I got them. But there was no time to think about this now. I was escaping death with one hand on the wheel.

As I parked and stepped out of the truck I noticed the glass cuts and bullet marks were gone. All that was left were the two mystery holes on my forearms and the large hole in my chest. Things were getting crazier and crazier. I have never wished for wounds on my body, yet I found myself hoping to find them. I took off the jacket and looked at my body in the rearview mirror, it was an embarrassing thing to do in public, but I didn't care. The marks were gone, my hopes for a logical explanation were evaporating.

At the front of the building I found a guy who was lost in a phone conversation. I waited with my hands tucked in the pockets of my jacket for him to finish. He was leaning against the building with his legs crossed. When he was through I asked him if he lived in that house. He indicated that he did, so I began to spin my tale of lies.

"I'm looking for a guy around here," I started.

"Name?"

"Mark Carson."

"Doctor Carson's son?"

"Yep, you know him?"

"Yeah, he's a friend of mine," he lied. I never knew this guy, I barely knew anyone in the neighborhood, but a lot knew me through my father. I kept playing.

"So where does he stay?"

"Used to live here once, father died in laboratory accident, no one heard of him since then."

"Just like that?"

"Yep, he just disappeared."

"But he lives here right?"

"Not anymore, the house was demolished after the accident. I think it was an explosion, who cares... anyway this new building was constructed after it."

"When exactly did this happen?"

"Two years ago."

I came here looking for an answers but I ended up with more questions. I was totally confused and frustrated. It was late, so I asked him if I could spend the night, he said no, I dug into my pocket and found some cash, I offered him twenty bucks and he grudgingly let me stay.

I slept on a small couch in his living room; it was a long day and I really needed rest but fate didn't want me to have some. A bad dream woke me up in the middle of the night; I had barely slept for two hours when I had to jump off of the couch. My nightmare wasn't as terrifying as what I saw after I woke up, the holes in my body, chest and arms, were glowing, I scrambled up off of the couch, screaming. I was lucky my roommate was a deep sleeper, and didn't hear me. The glowing finally stopped.

I couldn't take it anymore, I wondered if in the next minute I would have to start picking fallen parts of my body and attaching them to their right places. I thought about going to the hospital and about seeing a psychologist or Officer Patrick, yeah, Patrick Nelson would be a good idea, maybe all I needed was to speak to someone close.

Officer Patrick was a partner of my dad at Vegran City police department. He was dad's best and only friend since childhood. He was my friend as well. When I was younger I found it hard to differentiate between him and Dad; he came home with dad at night after duty, sometimes spent the night with us. I always wanted him to sleep with me in my room, he told nice bedtime stories and gave good advice.

Seeing Officer Patrick would be helpful in this kind of situation, he should be able to shed some light on what had happened.

I got dressed at dawn. My host was still asleep so I wrote a little note of appreciation and left it on the kitchen table when I left.

✶

At the Police Station, I climbed the stairs two at a time. On my way up I ran in to a couple cops I knew at VCPD, and exchanged a few words with them. They tried to console me about my father, but I didn't want to hear it, I didn't want to believe it. One of them told me where to find Officer Patrick; he was at the gun range.

About the same age with my dad, Patrick was still very handsome. I found him hitting the bull's-eye on some headshots. He took off his headset as he saw me.

"Are you losing your skills?"

"Are you out of sickbed already?" He said and smiled. He gave me a really tight hug, tears welling in his eyes, and we walked into an empty room.

"So how are you doing now?" He said, as I helped myself to a seat. He grabbed a chair and sat opposite me.

"I'm okay," I replied.

"I'm sorry about your dad."

"What happened to him?"

"What're you talking about?"

"I need an answer, Patrick."

"Wait, are you kidding?"

I explained to Patrick, told him I couldn't remember a thing. I told him that one minute I was on the lab bed and the other I woke up in the hospital. His face grew troubled as I finished my little story.

"Are you serious about this?"

"This can go on and on Patrick, just tell me what the hell happened."

After a long deep sigh, he narrated the tragedy of how my dad was murdered by Gordon. He said the cops got to our apartment after a couple of gunshots were fired. He led the team but Gordon and his men were long gone. He found Dad in the lab, on the floor, two bullets to the stomach, drenched in blood. And he found me on a lab bed with no injuries, but I was cold, unconscious. He knelt down before Dad with tears in his eyes as other cops called in the medics. Dad handed him a small black box. At this point of his story it sounded ridiculous, and I couldn't help but ask, "A box?" He nodded. He said I was rushed to the hospital immediately and that I've been in a coma ever since. The doctor said I was alive and would eventually wake, but he never said when. I could see joy written all over Patrick's face, he was happy to see me again.

He got off his chair and left the room, leaving me in more confusion. I started to rearrange the story in my head. My father was murdered by a criminal but the hospital claimed it was a laboratory accident. Something was definitely wrong. He came in a minute later slamming the door very hard behind him and handed me a box, a black box, the size of my hand.

"That's your father's last gift to you, son. Good luck," he said.

We had a drink and chatted for over an hour. He said Dad was already buried and that we would visit the grave someday. He offered me a place to stay. I thanked him, grateful my homeless days were over.

I left the police station hurriedly, without telling him about the strange things I've experienced since I left the hospital. I just drove away; I'll be talking about that later. My father last gift to me was a black box. Way to go Dad, this is no help. I was still unsure of what to expect from it, but I had to clear my head first.

At nightfall, I decided to stay in the truck after having dinner at Patrick's. It was cold and I wrapped myself in the jacket. I brought out the small box from my pocket, unlocked it and found a wristwatch. My life was growing weirder. I stared at it for over thirty minutes and then tried it on my left wrist. The watch turned on as I put it on, and started to blink. I was too carried away by the lights to check what was displayed on the screen, after a while it stopped blinking. It was still on and beeping, the light was exactly as bright as the one on my arm and chest, all of them gleaming in unison. The beeping became rapid and a hologram popped up from the wrist watch. It was Dad.

"If you are seeing this, son, you've probably seen some changes in your body."

"Yep," I murmured as he said that.

"That is the result of the cybernetic generator that I implanted in your body. Its enables your body to generate and create just about anything. It's connected to your brain which further enables you to generate and create weapons with merely a thought. Also it allows your body to heal rapidly and quickly."

"I see," I murmured again.

"Your abilities are powered by the molecules of your body, so it's not like it is going to run out of battery. As long as you still breathe, you have your powers. One more thing, with this wristwatch on you, I've designed a suit to ensure proper usage of your abilities. The suit has its own uses too. It's bullet-proof and indestructible and so is the wristwatch. Note that there is a limit to what you create, I think you can figure that out. Good luck son, the fate of the city lies in your hands."

I could sense that he was limiting the usage of too many scientific expressions, coming down to my level. The hologram blinked a few times and was gone. The wristwatch was still blinking, and as I stared at it, I started to feel relieved. I wasn't a freak after all.

I check the screen of the wristwatch and it read:

[Activate suit]

With curiosity I tapped the screen and the suit was generated. It started from my left arm where the watch was buckled, and spread to all part of my body, my face included. It felt like a colony of ants crawling on my skin and overwhelming me. At the arrival of the suit, I closed my eyes behind the mask, grit my teeth and clenched my fist, lost in the feeling of the great power that now resides in me.

The sight of Vegran city from the top of the tallest skyscraper was terrific. It is dark, and the city was at the peak of its beauty, lights everywhere: street lights, strobe lights, bulb lights, moon light. Nothing makes you feel much better than the view of such astonishing city of lights. Besides being so wonderfully colorful, the structure of the city is like no other, perfectly constructed skyscrapers, each having a unique shape and light coming from every window. Most workers in the city work really late, a really hardworking-population, another thing praiseworthy in Vegran city.

I shook myself out of the revelry over the city's beauty and turned my attention to its other side; the side that is like a beautiful demon. The dark side of Vegran city makes you want to cry till the end of days, crime and corruption in the city makes you want to die along with the victims.

Then I remembered Dad. I had earlier gone with Officer Patrick to his grave. Despite the fact that I was away, Patrick had been a good friend and he gave dad a decent funeral. For now, Patrick is the only one I can trust. At Dad's grave I was able to express my feelings too and I hope he heard me. I loved him, more than anything else, but he's gone now. I'll make sure he lives in my heart forever. And to do that, I'll have to continue what he had left unfinished. Vegran city is a beautiful girl, but with a dirty soul, her soul needs cleaning. There are no volunteers anywhere... I think it's time to get my hands dirty.

I looked down at the city from above; reflections of lights were visible on my black and white, cyber-generated costume. The mask covered from my eyes down to my jaw, leaving my forehead naked. My vision from the mask was technologically enhanced, and with it I can zoom in and out of the world before me, also I can calculate speed and actions precisely.

The glowing lights on my chest can light a dark room, but the ones my arms were gone, they only begin glowing when I try to use my abilities now.

Since the discovery of my power, I've been learning to utilize it perfectly. At the first, according to the projector on my lens, the percentage of my weapon generating speed and accuracy was twenty six percent, with practice, I have been able to increase it to fifty four percent, and with that I think I can handle some situations pretty well.

The built-in communication system in my suit beeped, the projector on the lens displayed:

[Incoming signal - Officer Patrick]

"What do we have officer?" I asked.
"Car pursuit, Collins street, can you make it?"
"Bet you I can."
"Just get your ass down here."
"Mind if I just 'drop' in?"
"Minimum damage please," he said and hung up.

I scanned the streets with my lens and located the pursuit; luckily the party was coming my way. I dove head first, spread my arms out wide and keeping my legs together as if flight was part of my abilities, but that doesn't mean I can't drop unhurt. It's time to save the night. Vegran city here I come.

★ EDWARD J. STINSON JR. ★

MILKMAN

MIL

FBI CRIMINAL FILE - THE MILKMAN

Subject Name: Milkman
Real Name: unknown
Alias: 'Tevvy', Tevye King (note - Tevye is the lead character from the movie 'Fiddler on the Roof')
Gender: Male
Age: 16-18 years of age

PHYSICAL ATTRIBUTES
Height: 5'5
Weight: 106 lbs (Thin Build)
Hair: Red
Eyes: Amber (he has been known to wears blue contacts which makes his eyes appear dark green)

Distinguishing marks: none
Distinguishing features:
His skin is milky white. His nails and tongue are naturally yellow. His breath is naturally rancid (smells like spoiled milk) so he is always eating mints. He sneers on the right side of his face (facing him) when he smiles.

PERFORMANCE
Abilities: Extraordinary memory for details.
Skill: Master serial killer with a meticulous nature.
Unique Traits: Extreme strength for his size (able to lift 300 lbs).

She was New to the Neighborhood

I visited her that night not so long ago. She was watching television.

She didn't know that I was in the closet beside her front door. In fact, she didn't know that I was in there all evening. I enjoyed watching that love story with her… even if I did it from the shadows.

She never made me bored, she giggled at the cute parts, cried at the sad parts, and topped it all off with a small carton of butter-pecan ice cream at the end. She made our friendship special.

She was new to the neighborhood and no one spoke to her.

The kids next door wouldn't even speak to her daughter as they passed by their front gate. I guess they didn't like little girls that still played with dolls. They didn't like little girls that waved to everyone. They didn't like new little girls in the neighborhood.

I wanted to help.

I decided to help.

That's why I like the shadows and the milk. They're both pure.

It wasn't until that night which made me realize how special our friendship really was. I couldn't wait to lick her face.

My father would be proud of me.

The first time I visited her house was yesterday. I left a bottle of milk in the closet. I left it to spoil. The same as she was doing to the neighborhood by being new.

The next night I entered through her patio window and waited in the closet with my milk. I uncapped it as a present for her to find.

She didn't search for the stench until her show ended and she finished her ice cream.

That was when she opened the closet and found me.

…

My father would be so proud.

Isaiah 60:16

—Milkman

FBI CRIMINAL FILE - THE MILKMAN

MENTAL MAKE-UP AND ANALYSIS

Personality: Dissociative, paranoid, and lonely. He misses society and knows not how to integrate.
Focus: To kill a family in key neighborhoods.
Purpose: To restore the bonds of community back to the 'old' days as he has learned from a stack of 1940's and 50's magazines that he was left with when he was a child.
Drive: He wants to prove himself to his abusive father, who makes up his second personality.

Summary: Tevye King (Milkman) firmly believes that he is a hero. His conservative beliefs are so deeply rooted in him that it has developed into an ideology equivalent to that of a religion. He has stated many times in therapy sessions that he was willing to die to save the, 'communities of old'.

HISTORY

FBI Notes - for his Historic details, the suspect will not be referred to as Tevye King, but instead as Milkman. Tevye King has been researched and clearly found not to be his real name. The following information has been organized from a total of three therapy sessions in which the final one resulted in a fatal assault upon the doctor and Milkman's escape.

Origin: His history is made up of fragments in which many components conflict. Milkman was apparently raised by his father in the hills of Tennessee; there are no records of his mother. It is believed that she left before his 7th birthday. His father knew that he was different and abused him as a way to direct the anger from the failures in his own life. His father was a failed delivery man.

According to Milkman, he grew up alone, learning how to read from an old chest of classic magazines. His father died sometime near his 10th birthday and Milkman survived in their mountain shack alone; he refused to identify the exact location. He stated that the dwelling was a little more than a dilapidated mobile home with a shabby wooden add-on bound to it to add an additional bedroom.

As his body continued to change in puberty, he developed a second personality which was populated by his father's anger. His skin became milky white and his eyes melded into a deep amber hue. (This was believed to be the results of a disease or ongoing illness. The medical results returned were negative to any known ailments on record. This is still being researched.)

Milkman became determined to become a hero to his father's rage by saving local communities as the delivery man of death. He found that communities came together whenever there was a slaughter of a family. It was his 'special' form of art.

He began to choose neighborhoods that he felt were 'broken' and studied them for the family that was most to blame. He particularly blamed single parent households. Once the family was chosen, he would systematically kill each one, often saving the mother for last. He stated that, he felt that she 'NEEDED' to watch because his mother left.

<u>Investigation Notes</u> - After each murder scene, the last one killed was found with Milkman's unique saliva dried across their face. He licked each victim from their lower jaw, across their cheek, and up to their hairline before killing them.

When asked about this, he had no answer and merely sneered.

He would always unplug the refrigerator and leave a bottle of open milk on the front porch to sour as time passed. According to him, it represented the evolution of communities and the souring of relationships.

On the walls of each home he would leave his tell-tale signature of, 'ISAIAH 60:16' in blood.

<u>THE SERIAL KILLER IN MR. CLOVER'S NEIGHBORHOOD</u>

Mr. Clover loved his pistachio ice-cream with chocolate bits added on top. He would eat a small cone of it and drink a fresh carton of milk when he finished it to lie to himself about health after given in to his weakness.

He loved his women young, bored, and 'taken' just as much as the lies he told to himself about his weight, his success, and his achievements. He would tell Tanya, the new wife down the street, that he was the one who got rid of the drug dealers in their community. He would visit her with a smile each Monday morning, after her husband left, as a courtesy... he just wanted to make sure that she was settling in to the neighborhood. It need not be mentioned, that as head of the Home-Owner's Association, this was a duty he took most seriously and 'intimately'.

His sin after each late-Monday escape from their rendezvous would be a Pistachio ice-cream treat topped with chocolate bits and a fresh carton of milk. He would get them both from the small Milk and Ice Cream truck that had start visiting their neighborhood not much longer than when pretty-little Tanya arrived.

The truck met him at the park every Monday as though it was his confirmation that each of his visits was a success and he could never be caught.

"How ya' doing today, Tevvy?" The older man would ask the young ice-cream truck attendant every week.

"Good, Mr. Clover. I'm doing good." He'd always answer. "How was it today, Mr. Clover? Y'know I gotta know. Did you see her today? What happened?"

The old man did as he had always done for the last couple of months that this had been going on. He'd look around carefully, lean against the ice cream truck, bite into his treat, and give all of the details to the youth listening intently with eyes wide open filled with awe.

The old man's whispers were rude and vulgar, topped off with lustful tales of his sexual prowess and superior smarts. He made it known that the married woman, seventeen years his younger, was kept happy by his performance and charisma.

Tevvy's pale white face dared to blush at the things he was told. He couldn't pull away from Mr. Clover's tales nor help but to idolize his confidence and charisma. Tevvy really liked him.

Each day after Mr. Clover finished his ice cream treat and stories he would depart with a comment about his own home, "Well, Tevvy, my boy... I have to get back to my wife, kids, and boring life. When you get my age, son, you'll realize that any Monday morning you get in the arms of a beautiful woman, other than your own, is as good as things get in life!"

With that comment and a wave from the ice cream and milk salesman, Tevvy, Mr. Clover would disappear back to his world as a hardworking husband and a loving father.

That was until he missed his visit to the ice cream truck one morning... and then another.

That was until rumors began to circulate through the neighborhood.

Comments around the ice cream truck were made about the 'loose' new young wife at the end of the block whose husband left her. Comments were made about Mr. Clover's children fighting at school and his wife stuck in a deep stupor of depression and medicine. News spread about their misery, fights, and failing marriage.

The grass in Mr. Clover's front yard grew, his tree limbs hung, and his pool was green. His car was home more often than not and his home became as much of an eye-sore as pretty-little Tanya's at the end of the block.

Tevvy knew he had to do something.

The pale youth prayed about it before action. He read scripture after scripture from his father's old leather Bible seeking guidance for his actions. There were so many verses on community and helping his fellow man, until he resolved that this was another one of the divine tests that he knew he had to pass.

It was a test... just like the others.

In his mind, he would be tested like this until he could change the world. He had to keep doing this until he learned perfection. Tevvy had to humble himself and to save something greater than him. He had to save Mr. Clover's neighborhood.

He knew to watch his home, because it was inevitable that one of their fights would make him leave. When it happened, it was nothing more of a repeat that he has witnessed so many times before. Mr. Clover barged out of the front door staggering to the door of his Buick and drove it down the street weaving from side to side as though death would be a blessing for him. Tevvy knew he had to act fast.

★

It was Mr. Clover's daughter's window that was open.

It was his youngest son that noticed him first; Tevvy's amber eyes gleamed against the shrouds of darkness as an interruption only second to sound. The older son challenged him, but that did not last long. A few bumps on the floor and walls, followed by the staleness of night time silence was enough to bring their mother to the top of the stairs.

She was important to Tevvy. It was important that she was last. No form of art... is art, without appreciation. No applause can ever be appreciated without the sound that comes from it.

Her grunts were delightful to the ice cream and milk salesman; her challenge and fight... almost erotic. Pulling her into the room, by her hair, with her 'silenced' children was more difficult than normal because of her size, not to mention that the floor was slippery.

Her scream... music.

This was the applause that Tevvy waited for.

It was from the heart and it was real. She screamed until exhaustion. Just beyond that Tevvy made her forever quiet. He showed his gratitude by lying with her amongst the children for all but awhile, and then slowly licked her face from her jaw line to the edge of her hair. For him, her tears were deliciously salty. This made him lay beside her for ten minutes more.

His clothes became a piece of his art as the purity of its white cloth took on the crimson hue from his handiwork. He carried a small bag with him down to the kitchen visiting each room in the house just to get to know Mr. Clover better. He just 'knew' that he would be proud of him. Stopping beside the sink, he shoved his hand against the wall and wedged the refrigerator plug from the outlet.

"Things are going to spoil now." He whispered to himself with glee.

Pulling his shirt off, he used it as a paintbrush to complete his canvas of art on the living room wall. He wrote:

'ISAIAH 60:16'

The youth opened the front door and pulled a bottle of warm milk from his bag. He opened it and left it on the porch beside the door before leaving. His walk through their driveway was more of a light dance as he began to sing nursery rhymes into the night.

He then stopped at the edge of the road as though he was interrupted and stared off to the side.

"What?" He asked. "I – I did it, Daddy. I did it. You don't have to keep at me for a while now. I helped this neighborhood, Daddy."

The pale youth jerked around quickly as though he was paranoid then looked back at the house, "See, Daddy, I made it pretty. It's like my ice-cream and milk. It's perfect. Mr. Clover don't have to be sad anymore. He can go with pretty-little Tanya now."

The boy stood straight, shifting his attention back to the street.

"I gotta go now. I did everything that I could. God gonna love me now, Daddy. He's gonna love me now; at –at least until next time."

He then ran to his small ice-cream truck and drove into the night.

This town would never forget the horrors left by… the Milkman.

FBI CRIMINAL FILE - THE MILKMAN

CRIMINAL RECORD:

Milkman is responsible for the deaths of 7 families across 4 states and 2 deputy officers, totaling 26 people.

The first time he was captured, he was behind a local convenience store in a small town located in Mississippi, licking a woman who he had just killed. He escaped the jail by killing the two deputy officers the next day. It was believed the officer attempted to 'question' him in his cell and were taken by surprise by Milkman's strength. This incident is currently being investigated.

He was recaptured three months later in North Carolina and ordered to psychiatric rehabilitation by the court. This resulted in Milkman's fatal assault upon his doctor and subsequent escape.

He has not been seen in over six months.

MILKMAN SHOULD BE CONSIDERED ARMED AND EXTREMELY DANGEROUS.

★ **QUINTIN BAKER** ★

BULLY

It was well after midnight when Latoya Johnson arrived outside of ASSets strip club. The place was a sleazy establishment that lay on the outskirts of the town. The building itself looked completely dilapidated, and all the neon lights and signs that covered the dirty walls, and windows made Latoya grimaced as she approached the entrance.

"You lookin' for a job babe?" The bouncer asked when Latoya walked up to him. The music that was blaring from inside the club was so loud that she almost didn't hear the question.

She didn't say anything for a few long moments. The question did not surprise her, her body was as alluring as any of the girls who worked inside, and she was not dressed conservatively. She wore a tight matte black jumpsuit with matching thigh high boots, and gloves. Her hair was tied in a black scarf and she wore large, dark sunglasses. A sword strapped to her back completed the disguise. Dressed as she was, at a place like this, she was bound to be mistaken for a performer. "Yeah," she lied. "Donnie told me to come over tonight so I could show him what I can do." She had planned to pay the cover to get in, and then work her way back to Donnie's office but, this seemed to be a much easier path.

"I'll bet," the bouncer replied, and he eyed Latoya lewdly. "Now what's your name darlin'? I'll tell em you're here."

"Bully," she responded, putting as much sexuality as she could behind the word.

The bouncer reached for a walkie-talkie clamped to his belt and raised it to his mouth. "Boss, I've got a girl named Bully out here. She says you told her to come by."

"I don't know no chick named Bully," a voice spoke through the walkie-talkie. The speaker sounded a bit aggravated to Latoya. "And I ain't tell nobody to come by here either."

"OK boss," the bouncer replied. He looked at Latoya and shrugged his shoulders helplessly. "Sorry sweetheart, but it don't look like you're gonna be showing anybody anything tonight. You can still come inside and enjoy the show if you want," he said, in an attempt to be compassionate. "And if you let me get your phone number I'll let you slide by for free." The man added, with a lecherous smile.

Latoya took a deep sigh, and turned away from the man for a couple of heartbeats before turning back to regard him once again. *"Looks like it's back to doing this the hard way."* The young woman thought to herself. She was just about to give the bouncer a wrong number when the boss's voice blasted through the walkie.

"Hey Vick, what does that chick look like?" He asked.

The bouncer looked over Latoya again for a long moment and seemed to be considering her description.

"Fine as hell," he said into the walkie, all the time smiling at woman in front of him. "She's got some kind of stripping ninja gimmick going, real original. She's worth taking a look at."

"Alright, I'm sending Lou down to get her," the boss responded.

"No problem boss," Vick clamped the walkie-talkie back on his waist and once again brought his attention to Latoya. "Well it looks like it's your lucky night after all," he said, still wearing the grin. "Listen, before my friend comes to get you, do you think I could still get your number?"

For a second Latoya considered it. Vick was tall, handsome, and well built. If the circumstances were different she may have given the man her phone number, just to see what he was really like. But the circumstances were not different. He worked for Donald Thompson, so he was the enemy, and if she had to, Latoya would leave him dead in the street.

"Maybe when I come back," she replied sweetly.

"OK," Vick said, nodding slowly and still smiling at the young woman. "Oh," he began abruptly, and he pointed a finger at Latoya's sword. "You can't take that thing inside. We don't allow weapons in the club. Sorry."

"But it's not even sharp," Latoya countered. "I just needed a prop to go with my outfit. Can't you let me slide by with it?"

"Sorry sweetheart, but I can't. Even if it's dull, you can still use it like a big metal stick." He quickly interjected, "Not you babe," and he put his hands up defensively trying not to raise the ire of the woman. "But if you put it down during your routine, and *somebody else* got a hold to it, then it's my ass, not yours. I can't take the chance."

Latoya reluctantly loosened the shoulder harness, and took out the sheathed sword. With a sigh, she handed it to Vick and her shoulders slouched. She had lied about the dullness of the sword; in fact, she had sharpened it herself earlier that morning. It was the only weapon she had thought to bring with her and she did not want to go inside without it.

She did not have much time to lament, as a burly man dressed in a cheap brown suit came out of the front door and stood next to Vick. He looked as though he had lived a rough life; his pink skin looked rough and leathery. His clean shaven face had old features that ran contrary to his oily black, combed back hair. He did not wear a tie and the top two buttons on his shirt were left open revealing a bush of salt and pepper chest hair that seemed to be trying to escape from the opening. A handgun was holstered openly on his left hip. Latoya thought he looked like a cliché guy from some 1980's gangster movie.

"This her?" He said, examining Latoya.

"Do you see any other gorgeous looking women out here?" Vick replied with has much sarcasm as he could muster. To accentuate the point he held his arms out wide and took an exaggerated look around the nearly empty street.

"Damn it Vick, why do you always gotta be a smartass?" The man said, clearly aggravated.

"'Cause Lou, you're always acting like a dumbass." Vick shot back.

Turning away from Vick, Lou looked at Latoya. "What's your name baby?"

"Bully," she said, adding a bit of sass to her tone.

"Well, Bully, I see my friend here wasn't joking about your looks," Lou began. "I'm gonna take you to see Mr. Thompson, and if he likes you, then you're in. And if you dance as good as you look, then you're gonna do good here.

Latoya nodded and smiled, her first sincere smile of the whole night. She indeed thought that she would well there, but it had nothing to do with her dancing.

Lou opened the door for her and followed her into the club. It was a dark, smoky place. The music seemed too loud and the floors did not look as though they had been cleaned in years. The space itself was huge. Three full sized dance stages complete with poles extended from the center of the back wall. Glass walls separated the three stages and the lounge areas around them into three, huge individual rooms. Every room had at least a score of drunken patrons clamoring over a naked, dancing woman on the stage. Latoya noticed that a few of the drunks were actually uniformed police officers. A bar area sat on the far right wall. Here too, a half dozen or so drunks congregated, dividing their attention between the strippers and the three big screen TV's showing highlights of the local sports team's earlier game. Outside the glass rooms several billiard tables were set up. Dim lamps hung from the ceiling, providing light the pool tables but not to the rest of the club. The three areas looked deliberately separated. The only constant was the deafening music that blared throughout the entire establishment.

Latoya stopped and waited for Lou, who quickly caught up and led her down the left wall of the club. Nearly half way down, the wall opened up to a set of stairs that ran up and down adjacent to the wall. Lou led the woman upstairs, noting that the downstairs path led to the private dancing rooms. She also took note of the security cameras in this section of the club. The two moved quickly up the stairs and down a short hallway, to a large wooden door. There were two guards protecting the door; one either side. They were both large white men wearing black dress shirts, and slacks, and brandished firearms on their waists. One was bald with a goatee; the other was clean shaven with short bleach blonde hair.

Lou opened the door, and held it as Latoya entered. He closed it after her, and moved to stand near the door on Latoya's right. The room was quiet, obviously sound proofed, much to her relief. The office was larger than Latoya had expected. The large wooden desk dominated the space in the center. To her left a row of file cabinets stood against the wall. To her right was a huge glass bookshelf filled with all types of books. After a cursory glance at the room, she shifted her focus to the man sitting behind the desk looking at a laptop screen. He was Donald Thompson. He was the man Latoya had come here to kill.

Donald's hair was gelled and combed neatly back. His skin smooth and tanned to a perfect bronze. He had a goatee, shaved quite sharp. The man wore an expensive designer business suit that was black with gray pinstripes. He also wore an elegant black and gray wrist watch. He had the look of a Wall Street CEO, not a lowlife strip club owner, or a wannabe mob boss.

Latoya looked at him intently. This was a mask, she thought to herself. Donald Thompson was no man; he was a monster who had raped her little sister, beat her half to death, and left her body on their parents front lawn early one morning. He may have looked like an upstanding member of society, but Latoya could never see him as anything other than an animal. An animal that needed to be put down.

Donald looked up from the laptop and smiled when he saw the very alluring woman standing before him.

"So," he began. "You want to be a dancer in my club, huh? Well, you've got the look. I need to see if you can dance though."

He moved his hand over to a knob on the desk, and turned it. Slowly the music from the club began to fill the office through speakers built into the walls.

Latoya felt her heart racing. Fear and excitement swirled inside of her as the moment of truth neared. She sighed deeply to steady herself, and buried all of her nervousness, and doubt under a mountain of rage. Rage forged from all the pain that this man had caused her family.

"I didn't come here to dance," she said, with a face that could have been made of stone.

"What?" Donald asked, his eyebrows drawn together in confusion.

"I came here to see the man who raped and beat my sister."

"What the hell are you talking about?" Donald asked again, still trying to get a grasp on what was happening.

He looked to Lou for answers but the old gangster could only shake his head and shrug his shoulders.

"Does Denise Johnson ring a bell?" Latoya asked, and hate was clear in her voice as well as on her face.

"Oh," Donald began, and he nodded with a growing understanding.

"That bitch that was gonna rat me out. You're her sister. Let me tell you something; I was going to pay her a lot of money to keep her trap shut, but she wanted to be a goodie-goodie. So she got what goodie-goodies get."

Latoya clinched her fists tightly, remembering how she talked her sister out of taking the money. She told Denise that it's her responsibility to tell the truth and put men like Donald Thompson behind bars, where they belong. It was she who gave her sister the strength to go back to Donald and refuse his offer. But Donald Thompson did not take no for an answer; so he gave her one last warning; a warning in the form of a brutal rape and savage beating. The family tried to go to the police afterwards, but it was soon very obvious that the club owner had paid off all the right people to make the problems go away.

Donald looked at Latoya with cold, uncaring eyes. Hers blazed with a fire and hatred that could not be sated.

He reclined in his seat. "Now you come down here," Donald said, "Trying to get revenge on me, in my own club. Just like a goodie-goodie. I think it's time YOU got what goodie goodies get." He nodded at Lou.

Lou moved to grab Latoya from behind, but before he could grab her, she lashed out with a vicious elbow that caught the old man squarely in the diaphragm. The air exploded out of him. He was about to double over when another elbow struck, this one was aimed higher, at the man's throat. A flash of triumph flared in her heart as she felt the gangster's wind pipe collapse under the weight of her strike. The old man fell to the floor holding his throat and trying to gasp for air that would not come. As he fell she grabbed the gun that was holstered on his hip.

His downward motion allowed Latoya to pull the gun free with ease. Before Lou ever hit the ground she had the weapon up and trained on Donald who was going for something under his desk. After seeing his only ally in the room put down and a very angry woman pointing a gun at him he thought better of making any quick moves. Instead he raised his hands up to his shoulders.

"I guess you're not a goodie-goodie," he said, as he watched Lou thrash violently several more times, and then suddenly lay very still.

"Let me see the laptop," she said, ignoring the statement.

He complied, reaching out with one hand to turn the laptop to face Latoya. She saw that the screen was divided into a grid with several smaller screens, each one displaying the feed from a different camera.

"I don't think you've thought this through thoroughly." Donald said, calmly. "There are two guys on the other side of that door that will hear the gun go off, and after they kick the door open there goes the sound proofing. If you get into a firefight with them, I got at least six other guys in the club and two cops that work for me in the building. There is no way you're getting out of here alive."

"You don't have to worry about me, you piece of shit," Latoya replied, as she moved towards the wall opposite of Lou's corpse. "Besides, aren't you feeling light headed?"

"What are you..?"

Before he could finish Latoya fired. The bullet hit him just above the bridge of his nose. Blood and brain matter plastered on the wall behind him as his lifeless body fell back into the seat. A few heartbeats later the two guards burst into the door. They froze for a moment, shocked to see their employer's brains decorating the walls. The moment was too long. Before the two could regroup enough to get their weapon, and ready for a threat Latoya was on them. She struck the nearest goon (the bald one) barbarically with the barrel of the gun, and then pushed him into his partner. The Blonde guard tried to back up in hope of avoiding his dazed and stumbling friend, and find room to aim at her. All hope of that plan vanished as he fell backwards over Lou's dead body, and his partner crashed on top of him. Latoya rushed to the door, and slammed it shut. In a sound proof room so far away from the club floor, no one heard her fire off fifteen shots into the guards.

A few moments later a woman wearing all black walked out of ASSets strip club with a leather laptop case on her shoulder.

"Well, how did it go?" Vick asked, apprehensively.

"Not good," she replied. "I don't think he liked me. Can I have my sword back?"

"Sure," he said with a smile, and handed the weapon back the woman.

She unsheathed, and admired it in the neon lights. "Thank you," she said in a soft voice.

"No problem," Vick replied. "But, can I still get your number?"

"I'm sorry, I already have a boyfriend," she lied. "It's probably better if you forgot you ever met me."

"Girl, you know I'm not ever gonna be able to forget you," he responded.

Latoya looked around cautiously to make sure no one was watching.

"OK, I'll give you something to remember me by." She reached up stroked his hair, and kissed him sweetly. She felt her heart sink when Vick jerked and pulled away to see her sword protruding from his belly. He looked at her with blood trickling from his mouth, his eyes pleading for an answer to why she had done this.

"I'm sorry," she said, as he fell to the ground. "But you were the only one left who could identify me, and I couldn't risk you putting my family in danger."

She wasted little time in extracting the sword and wiping the blood on Vick's shirt. With the sword, and laptop strapped to her back, Latoya disappeared into the backstreet of Deer Run, satisfied that she had avenged her sister and made the world just a little bit better.

★ EDWARD J. STINSON JR. ★

THE VEIL

"We are tha breath of fear and their vision of terror. We hated them ten generations past, and tha pyres that have burned from that vengeance, continues to burn within us today," states the hard-worn battle fatigued elder sitting on a wet stump.

The hell-night heat seems not to affect him as his raspy voice chants purpose and origin through words of experience.

"I hate the deep-skins! They ain't natural to this world and they ain't natural to mortals. We wasn't ever meant to be one with 'em, and that's why we was created." He pauses from sharpening his sword and uses his calloused hand, holding his whetstone, to wipe the sweat from his brow. His face is scarred and his stare piercing.

"A demon's a demon. Ain't no separatin' them. Ain't no understandin' them. Killin' them is gotta be done and that's what we do."

He inspects his blade's edge amidst the deep night and the glare of the crimson moon. Upon approval of its potential to serve him as his personal gift of death, he sheathes it slowly without sound and breaks the shadows to lean forward towards the three youths squatted before him.

"Each of you is special. None of you got nobody, cause of them deep-skins. Each of you lost your family to them. Because of that loss, each of you was handpicked for our team. Each of you was chosen by a cursed-blessing to be a demon-killer, know that I serve Jaeh'ru faithfully and when he speaks to me, he tells me to find the likes of you to make the best harbingers of death that could be bred from his whispers." He fans the gnats away from his face and stands before the focused youths.

"Tonight, the Blood Moon serves us! Tonight we killin' deep-skins!"

Donned in moist leather attire, nothing worn by the strong-jawed hunter was anything but functional. His inner shirt dank with sweat, was new-dirt gray and patched together from rags of the poorest of corpses found and forgotten on the most distant roadways and battlefields. His pants were loose fitting and pocketed in unlikely creases to hide tools of a master thief and weapons critical to the cornered assassin. His belt is a piecemealed mess of pouches and rope which has served him on more than a few missions of death against his sworn enemy, the demons. His musk was that of an unkempt mortal and a bathless hound; it is unmistakable to any demon seeking to hunt his existence. All of these were his tools.

A tear along the breeze only far enough away to define the edge of the clearing surrounding the leader and his three youths carries a heed through the voice of another veteran warrior returning from his scout.

"Agodrian, we have to move. The deep-skins are coming and the Blood Moon thirsts."

The elder acknowledges by melding into the darkness behind him. His new followers respond with imitation as the shadows welcome them with an embrace of cold. They have learned to read the edges of light that dance within all forest darkness, for it is one of their first lessons of the hunt. A demon's vision is that greater than any mortal during the daylight when the moons have risen and the sky is blackest. From this their confidence is without question and their awareness is blurred into arrogance; for those of the Veil, it is this lesson that is taught during their acceptance beyond initiation. It is a critical part to defeating these unholy beasts.

Agodrian motions from his position as he dons the final components of his guise. He tugs quickly, whipping his cloak to a close, creating the fluttering sound of an evening bird moving into the sky with intent for travel and less for fear. He kneels as he pulls the strange durable cloth lying around his neck into place above his nose and mouth. He exhales through it and the cloth responds with uneasy life, pulling firm into a mask which acts as his veil. His personal darkness becomes that much more while waiting on his prey.

It is the musky stench which elevates from his position that dances on this hot night's humid breeze. The applause from this entertainment is given by the realization of three soldier demons flying by on patrol who detect the scent and hones in for search. It is the husky leader that lands first wearing a shroud of wolf leather with slices of gold ripped across his shoulders as a reminder of rank. He grunts to the other demons with strong nudges against their wings to direct their searches into key areas. His orders are lowly gurgled and snarled in demon tongue which adds to the anxiousness of those hunting them.

The gruff voice revives memories in each of them of past attacks and family loss. For the youngest, barely twelve terans old, he begins to sweat as memories stab at his soul, as he relives the thought of his mother burning alive from a demon standing on her throat during the collapse of his torched home. He hid under the floorboards and watched her pain become numb as her flesh boiled around the final word from her blistered mouth, "Mikal."

It was his name.

Giving up from their lackadaisical search, the leading demon grunts against a laughing cough and waves his fellow demons over to a small fire that he is creating from Banta-stone and flint. When clacked together the Banta-stone ignites into a determined flame that feeds from the stone itself. It's excellent for burning mortal villages with sweeping passes from the sky, but tonight it is just right for cooking some wide breast four-winged chicken that he was carrying in his food satchel.

Hunger and anticipation crawls over the pair of demons returning to their leader as a heavy 'THUNK' reminds one of them the difficulty of life and living when a breath cannot be taken. He looks down from the stunted impact through his back and wastes a mouthful of blood on top of the spear shaft clearly piercing his back left wing and exiting through his lung. His armor only served as a weight to aid in his quick fall to the ground from the start of a well-organized ambush.

"THE SHADOWS ARE ALIVE!!!" Cries the partnering soldier demon in common tongue.

The leader stumbles over his open flame as his leather wings flap haphazardly while trying to regain his balance. He attempts to regain control of the situation through command, but is silenced as a silhouette crosses above him in a leap with a cloak fluttering in the wind. The scent throws him off as it returns as demon-scent attached to mortal movements. The soldier demon raises his clawed-hands to guard against the landing hatred, but finds friendless fury as his attacker's war hammer slams through his forearm while finding placement into his skull by entering through his face. The brutal crunch of the blow is followed by an eerie sticky slush as the soldier demon falls to the ground as a vine chopped from the top of a tree. His death was pitiless as the attacking cloaked shadow holding the war hammer whips around to stare into the face of their final prey. It is then when recognition falls upon the leader, from stories hushed amongst the most meager demon guards and the mightiest demon warlords alike. It is a name with no allowance to be spoken for fear of creating myth, legend, and horror alike; but tonight this title finds life within an unholy-beast not known for trepidation.

"T-The Veil," mutters the final demon in common tongue.

Screeching as a trapped hawk, the demon jets into flight seeking escape through the canopy of the forest trees which border the heavens on the crimson streaked black sky. A ruffle from the adjoining bushes and a sharp snap giving way to the twang of branches flicking through tree forks moving up, releases a large net drenched in young snapberry jelly. The demon flies deep into the embrace of the net which tangles his wings and promises the cruel touch of gravity as he slams into the ground after flinging wobbly in a large arch across the forest floor. Each bump of the ground is followed with a strong 'HUNF!' until broken wing bones and deep lacerations transform his sounds into groans.

Five silhouettes detach from the clasp of the forest shadows and approach the broken demon, still struggling against the net. He is terrified. Agodrian places himself before his enemy and kneels to look into his eyes.

"We are the Veil, deep-skin," he says softly while unsheathing his sword.

He then rises up and scans for fear among the youths. The oldest one proved himself by throwing his spear into the back of the first demon. The second demon was killed by the other veteran scout warrior that reported their approach. This kill would have to be carried out by Mikal, the youngest member, or by the final member who was seventeen and the son of a Spiritualist, a holy man. Agodrian holds the handle of his sword out and makes his choice.

"Lehr. Come to this accursed beast and end his unholy existence."

The Spiritualists son moves forward to grab the hilt of the sword and hesitates.

"Th-This is wrong. I can't do this… I know that d-demons killed my family, but this won't make things right. P-Please forgive me, Agodrian, but I can't do this."

"I CAN!" Says the twelve teran old youth behind him, pushing

forward to grasp the sword hilt from Agodrian.

"Mikal, NO! Don't..." shouts Lehr as his young team mate buries Agodrian's sword blade into the throat of the netted demon.

He pushes and pushes with his small arms until the entire blade is sunk through the top of the demons throat down to the hilt of the sword. The broken flow of blood and air escaping from the dying enemy attempts to form words but fails to the impending darkness of death. Young Mikal does not blink.

He releases his grasp only after pulling the sword from the corpse and handing it back to Agodrian. He then stands before his taller teammate, Lehr, and spits in his face.

"They killed my family, Lehr. I will kill every damn demon that I see."

Lehr wipes his face slowly as he starts to cry. "Mikal, look what this is making us... making you. We can't-,"

Suddenly, Agodrian's sword blade erupts from Lehr's chest as he is stabbed from behind. His legs weaken and his head shakes as his neck muscles tighten. He grips the blade with both hands using all of his strength only to have his fingertips nearly severed as the blade is ripped backwards out of his body. Lehr falls forward onto his face as Mikal steps to the side a single pace to watch his final plummet, escorted with a fleeting death throe. Lehr dies slowly in the mud.

Agodrian wipes his blade on the body. "We'll gut these deep-skins and turn the flesh into cloaks. The cloaks are fire proof, touched against magic, and hide the smell of mortals. Each of you has earned a cloak," says the hard-worn elder while sheathing his sword. "The inner skin will be peeled away for you to use to hide your face. The inner skins of demons don't really ever die. When you breathe through it, the stuff makes your senses sharper and helps you to breath underwater."

He then kicks the demon to ensure that he is dead and looks back to his new team.

"Gentlemen,
welcome to the Veil!"

★ SUZANNIE M. LAWRENCE ★

NYTE'S TOY

The stale meat was attracting too many flies and swatting them became a chore. The wench that doubles as the inn's barmaid and nightly entertainment knew it was stale before she threw it on the fire pit, but because it was served to daemons, she knew they would stomach it.

A daemon swats at the swarm of flies before he turns to the innkeeper, Hekto.

"The flies 'er too many Hekto, have the wench set so'more smokers on this here side to drive 'em out." The Daemon points to his corner of the inn with a large dirty hand. "Spiked horns of the Dark One!" He swears to his Dark Godren T'Nae Hel. "The maggots'll fester before I can finish."

That's how it was in most taverns. Endaerian mortals are of soft delicate flesh, easy to tear with sharp talons and easy to make ill. While the T'Naebra demon breeds have three layers of thick skin to endure the heat and molten soil of their own world. Almost never able to become ill from mortal ailments, daemons eat meat and stored foods, even when it is considered to have gone bad according to mortal taste. At first it seemed insulting and the merchants who hated their kind hoped to sway them from frequenting their establishments, until it was discovered that it was indeed the preferred way to eat it, besides being freshly cut from the prey.

Hekto wipes his greased hand in the brown rag he was using to dry out the ale mugs, and snaps his pudgy fingers to get one of his barmaids' attentions.

"Grab two more smokers and be sure to stuff in enough of the herb mix to last the rest 'o the night." He winks at her and she shakes her head.

Holding out her hand, Hekto tosses the keys hooked to the loop on his apron at her. Keys that opens the locked room, inside the storage room. All the workers at Hekto's Inn knows he is a cheap bastard, and winking after barking out a command loud enough for the patrons to hear is his way of giving his signal for, 'you better not use too much'.

She sucks her teeth and continues to the storage room to get his concoction of herbs that is mixed to make the fly repellent he uses and sells to others. Not his invention, but that of his son, Jenner. A Druid at the Academy of Sigils, his son is one of the Academy's most gifted magic users and an Herbalist instructor. At first disappointed in his son's interest in magic, then finding out his son is indeed a Sigil, Hekto was reluctant to even have the boy visit in his robes. Until the visit when his son brought him the smoker. His invention at the Academy for foul smelling spells and experiments. Jenner would bring his father new smokers each visit and eventually Hekto found a way to profit by selling them to other Inns.

Jenner never divulged his part in the invention, nor the ingredients of the smoker, hoping one day to make his father proud. Grounded to a fine powder, the mix of herbs including Lavender, Mint, Basil, Bay Leaf, and Rosemary is made with an essential oil that drives many of the insects away. Hekto was just happy to have an upper hand on the other establishments.

As the woman walks through the Tavern area of Hekto's Inn she squeezes through the crowd of men watching a belly dancer, scantily clad in no more than flowing jewels, toned silks, and coined strewn fringe. As the lithe girl moves in and out of the throng of drunk and enthralled men and daemons, her suggestive movements stay in tune with the music. Her long golden hair flowing, her skirt swirling, and her hips keep them all unaware of the other barmaids emptying their ale mugs, assuring they reorder more of the taverns supply of drink.

The barmaid known as Nyte is new to Hekto's, and her responsibilities, so far, are limited to only running errands for the rotund innkeeper and resupplying the Dragon's Breath drink the inn is famous for. Only two things are kept locked away beyond the storage room and only Hekto has the keys for the room. The Dragon's Breath ale and the smoker's herbs. Aside from Hekto's Inn, only the Caramel Rolls at The Feathered Horse Inn are more famous in Saenia. Hekto's relationship with the Headmistress from the Citadel of Magic who runs The Feathered Horse has gotten better since Jenner became a respected student and although the competition between them has died down, Hekto is still wary of spies out to steal his secret recipes.

Nyte enters the storage room and as she ties a ribbon in her hair, her sharp eyes peer over her shoulder on the lookout, not for recipe stealing spies, but for wondering eyes, who might see her retrieving her dagger from her Mannasphere. She pulls out a small glowing green orb and swipes it along the edge of her blade. The liquid in the orb is quickly absorbed onto the blade's edge as the orb disappears with the liquid. She peers over her shoulder again when she hears a sound in the main storage room and finishes her preparation. She grips her dagger firmly one last time, anxious, before vanishing it into the magical realm created by her Mannasphere. She grabs the smoker's herbs and leave.

As Nyte enters the bar once more, she quickly glances across the room at a hooded man sitting in the far corner of the bar. Many sentences are silently spoken in that brief glance between the two as Nyte's game for the night has begun.

As she tosses the keys back to Hekto and places the smoker's in the corner, she does so in full view of the vile daemon who requested them, occasionally meeting his black eyes with a shy smile. The daemon tears a piece of meat with his hands, and bite into the meat, eating a few flies, mold and some dried blood. As he chews, he gives her a lustful look.

"Want to play a game, big boy?" Nyte asks the daemon.

"What games from our demon's world do ya know, wench?" He grabs a chunk of bread and sops up the bloody juices from the plate.

Nyte saunters over to the daemons table and as he raises the blood soaked bread, she licks it.

"I know many of the demons games from Tenaebra." She leans into his neck and bites him ferociously.

The daemon holds still and lets her release him before he smiles and leans back in his chair.

"Ya, I've got a good game for a wench like ya," he says, as Nyte walks away.

Nyte works her way to the other side of the Inn, picking up dirty mugs and plates from tables. As she reaches the hooded man's table she slows her task and takes a bit longer.

"I found my toy, so I can play my game." She says in a low voice.

"Are you sure you found the perfect toy for your game," the man responds as he continues to sip on his goblet of red wine.

"Yes. I will be playing soon. While I'm gone, you should say hello to the innkeeper." A quick look at Hekto and then the man makes her smile.

"I'm here to work, and so are you. Get to work and stop keeping me here longer than I want to be."

Self-consciously he lowers his hood a bit more and casually recast his cloaking spell to meld into the shadow further as she leans over to wipe clean his table.

"Since I've been here, he's mentioned your name at least three dozen times. Mostly to brag about your position at the Academy. He considers you a hero. He's very proud of you." Nyte pauses and looks Jenner directly in the eyes. "And he admires you as much as I do."

Jenner stares back at her. Feeling the pull he's always felt for her, he quickly opens his mouth to speak, closing it just as quickly.

He reaches for his goblet. Places it at his lips and with great disdain responds. "You're a Shade for the Shadow Communion." He takes a sip and swishes the liquid in his mouth. "You're their

assassin and occasionally a whore."

He swallows, hoping to wash down the bitter words.

Nyte's face twitches and the corner of her mouth crinkle into a mask of anger, which then slowly turns into a smile.

"Jenner, I am a whore when I am assigned to be. Just as you are." She glances over her shoulder as she leans closer, finally reaching close enough to see the fullness of his face. "You want me as much as I want you. And whore, assassin, or Sigil, whatever we are for the Shadow Communion, our loyalty is to the Royal Family." Nyte licks the tip of his nose. "Just as my body's loyalty..."

"Stop it," he interrupts her and turns his face away. "Do your job."

Nyte eases back. "Yes. I will." She leaves his table with a grin.

Jenner watches her walk away as the resentment of his attraction for her is as a bitter herb to chew. But one that he does often.

As the tavern empties out and the daemon has had enough of being teased by Nyte, he gathers his belongings and waves a large hand through the air at Hekto.

"I'm headed to 'ma room, send 'yer barmaid up with ma food." He points directly at Nyte, making sure Hekto sees his selection.

He rises, shifts his sword belt into place, takes one last chunk of meat, flies and all, into his mouth and washes it down with his last sip of Dragon's Breath.

As he begins to climb the steps at the back end of the large room, now almost empty, save for a few stragglers after a bustling night of business, he pauses.

"Hekto, tell the wench I want to play." He smiles a sadistic toothy smile and continues to his room down the darkened hall.

Hunting is always fun, especially when you get to toy with the prey before the kill. Nyte thinks to herself as the remaining tavern visitors start to finish off the last of their Dragon's Breath ale the tavern is famous for, and as the barmaids transform into savory delights to satisfy more carnal appetites. The drunken men and women laugh and take pleasure in the room as their actions are obscured by the smokers used to keep bugs and other pest out. Hekto tosses a dirty rag over his shoulder and slaps Nyte on her rump as she passes by him carrying a tray.

"Get your pretty ass over there and tidy up those table lass, you haven't got all night. That daemon's waiting in his room for his bisque and some service, and he's never a patient one."

Nyte looks over her shoulder giving the inn keep a teasing and seductive wink.

"Maybe I'm hoping to spend tonight servicing another, Hekto." Her smile and dark eyes, intensified by her dark curly hair held up by ribbons.

Hekto, aged and once a seasoned soldier, now content with his life serving adventurers and fighters much younger than he when he ventured out, rather enjoys hearing stories told to him as he once told in his youth to the old tavern keep he acquired the place from. Feeling flattered at the thought, he knows she jests or speaks of another. But an old man can hope. He can hope that one day he meets a woman who wants him, simply because he is Hekto and not the well-to-do owner of a tavern. His graying beard and balding head masks his bashfulness that makes his boyish charm apparent. Masked from many with an untrained eye, but not the shadowed figure sitting in the corner since early evening. A shadowed figure that has eyed the Innkeeper since his entrance and that of Nyte since the start of her shift, as well as the tables she has served.

As Nyte removes her apron, she tosses it at another barmaid taking her place, as she adjust her bodice to show more skin and the ample breasts she boasts. Hekto watches her intently, almost sadly. He knows how rough and forceful daemons can be, and this one, having been at the inn two nights, had been ruthless with the last girl. Reminding Hekto to have someone check on her since she has been out sick since.

When Nyte climbs the steps at the back end of the large room and smiles a quick smile at him, Hekto feigns a guilty smile, not noticing her quick look at the hooded man.

A soft knock is greeted with a gruff voice as she opens the door meekly to a darkened room.

"Come, I waited long 'enuff fer 'ya wench." The voice rises with slight frustration. "What cha think, I'd wait 'ere all night."

With no other furniture adorning the room save for a chair facing the bed and the food table, the dark colors of the sheets and dimly lit candle in the middle of the room would have obscured her view of the daemon on the bed. Almost.

"I have your bisque, and it's still very hot." She puts the tray of bisque on the table. "We can play while it cools."

"Git over 'ere and strip, I wan'ta see 'yer body 'fore I offer 'ye any compensate." The daemon spits out some crumbs as he speaks.

Moving with enough sultriness to get the daemon to sit up in the bed, Nyte unties her bodice, smiles shyly, and sashays between the bed and chair, using the arm of the chair for support to lean over and give him a good view of her body. Moving her hips in a snakelike motion she slips out of her bodice and shimmies out of the olive colored frock she wears. Her naked body continues her dance of enticement as she looks over her shoulder.

"Do I please you?"

With only his smile as confirmation she faces the chair and lifts her right leg slowly resting it on the seat of the chair. Arching her back and leaning forward, she accentuates her rump in the dim light. Slowly bending over far enough to look between her parted legs, she rubs her hands up and down her legs and rump as she coils her back and shoulders enticingly to the soft sounds of music coming from the tavern below.

"Yer one 'o dem harlots that got skills. What's 'yer name."

She laughs and turns to face the daemon as she releases her dark curly hair from the ribbons and pins holding it up. Her locks fall short just above her firm breasts giving a nice frame to her nipples, hard from the cool night air.

"I am called Nyte." She glides gracefully toward the bed her arms tucked behind her back pushing her chest forward.

The daemon pushes forward to greet her at the foot of the bed where he sits up letting her stand in front of him.

"I will serve you, however you wish," she adds, twirling a lock of her hair.

He looks over her body as his burly hands move across her skin. He grabs her rump in both hands and pulls her forward into his face, inhaling deeply as he sits on the edge of the bed.

"Smells nice too." He licks her stomach from her navel up and over her left breast, stopping to take her nipple in his mouth.

He does not see her face as she looks up at the dark ceiling with disgust, swallowing what anger is building in her. Anger, not from the fact that her body is being violated, but by the fact that a demon is masquerading as a daemon on Endaeria.

A demon. They do not believe in the forgiveness of the Celestial. They have forsaken their Aeon master, Luciphaer, and turned to the ways of the Dark Godren Lord, T'Nae Hel. T'Nae the Godren of War and Destruction.

The demon grabs her arms fiercely and pins them behind her back, twisting her and tossing her on the bed forcibly, causing her to shriek in surprise.

"Sweet." He dives into her body, again holding her down licking her breast and biting her skin.

Nyte screams and struggles under the demon. "Wait, I'm going to give you what you want, you don't..."

Her protest is silenced by a slap across the mouth and heavy hands tightening fingers around her neck. She gasps for several seconds then realizing air has stopped coming, she lifts her leg slightly bending them at the knees to get her footing on the bed. As trained reflex kicks in, she raises her hips and presses against the demons crotch as he straddles her, and she feels him hard with his crazed lust. Like an arrow slips through a chink in armor, she accurately slips her hands between his forearms breaking his chokehold.

Caught off guard, the drunken demon responds too slowly to stop her from twisting her body with feline grace to flip onto her stomach. Pushing off the headboard, Nyte slides down the bed between his legs with exercised proficiency to come up behind him.

"I wasn't gon'ta hurt ya," he says as he spins around to reach for another grab.

He is met only by the gleam in front of his face caused by the candle reflecting off her blade. His throat feels cool from the night air and then he feels warn liquid flow down his bare chest. His throat constricts and he finds it hard to talk. His head bobs back and forth from the blur of his vision. He reaches out his hands grasping at her, as her beautiful, naked, sweet smelling body backs up. The taste of her flesh on his tongue is now mixed with another taste. One he knows too well. One he would have tasted had he the chance to sink teeth into flesh like he had done with so many other women before her.

"You would have killed me." Picking up her frock and wiping her blade efficiently, Nyte confesses with her back to him. "You would have killed me and feasted on my flesh like you did with the others. Demon."

She runs her finger delicately over her blade and uses her magic, gifted by her half-mortal blood, to vanish it again. Grateful for the few spells she knows and able to use in her trade, she is most grateful to Jenner for teaching her to cast Mannasphere. The ability to manipulate Manna and objects, making magic user's able to discretely carry many needed items.

Nyte turns to face him. "Your kind is why the mortals hate us. You eat flesh like the savages our people once were. The Storms sent you, didn't they demonspawn?" Nyte says with a scowl on her face.

The demon clutches his throat gurgling. Looking around the room like a cage animal as his life seeps onto the dark sheets the anger in his eyes burn, causing the cursed bloodrage to take hold.

"Your bloodrage will not help you, demon. The blade is tainted." Nyte holds her blade out in front of her face, an evil grin graces her victim. "The poison is enhanced to weaken." She sits in the chair watching him with trained tenacity.

"Bloodrage is of the old ways, the strength you gain is that of a corruption and foulness. Not welcome here in Kalöt. It is forbidden."

Her pagan eyes shift to the door of the room as she hears light scratching. "It's done," she speaks.

The door opens slightly and a shadowy figure slips into the room. The figure stands in the shadows at the doorway silent when he sees the demon still alive, now slumped and twitching.

"He's almost gone. He tried summoning bloodrage. Only prolonging the inevitable. I wasn't able to play with this one. Tried to choke me before he raped me," Nyte says rising from the chair bending slightly to look into the demons eyes as his final breaths are fought for. "I would have shown you a great time before I gutted you. You ruined it for both of us, demonspawn."

The man removes the hood showing his handsome features. "My father is looking good. Still selling smokers and skimming on the herbs I see."

Nyte smiles. "You should say hello. He misses you." She says in a song-like coo, eyeing him for some emotional reaction.

She sees none.

"Come, I'm done here. Let's report." She reaches out as Jenner hands her a cloak.

Nyte wraps herself, shrugging off the chill air and looks up to see Jenner looking down sadly.

"Since I became a Hexen, my skill at raising the dead is far more sinister than mixing herbs to impress him... Hunting and killing living things. He would shun me again. I... I'm just happy to know..."

Nyte reaches up and kisses Jenner on the lips, cutting him off mid-sentence.

"One day... ole Hekto will accept you... as you are... and you will have me... as I am." She chooses her words carefully.

The two Shades look at each other intensely as death enters and leaves the room with the concluded breath of the demon.

"I'm still in the mood to play," Nyte breaks the silence.

The Sigil's face is a cold mask. He reaches out a hand and looks over her shoulders at the demon.

As they walk away he tells her, "Nyte, you can't toy with the prey before you kill it."

★ **KARL JOSEPH** ★

ARCLIGHT

I hate superheroes.

No, I really do. Whether it's the government brownnosers or the corporate pansy elite, one thing's clear: they all suck. Swift Striker's way too mainstream and is more a one-man boy band than an actual superhero with his debut album of what he likes to call "Super-Pop" (gag me), Hyper Womyn is annoying with her smug sense of feminism and constant petitions for every registered female costumed crusader to receive a statue in Washington, and don't even get me started on Smithson-Ion. One fact remains ever present in our wonderful world and economy: supes' and their neurotic baddies can all take a long walk on a short pier.

Which is why when I had my First Awake (or as Senator Buckley calls "Meta Gene discovery happening") I spazzed for near twenty minutes, broke several holes through my room's plaster, and seceded from my family.

People always said, "Boy, Glen, you sure have a glow about you!"

Little did I know that glow would decide to manifest itself in my fingertips one chilly September night, but manifest itself it did. At first it was really subtle; I thought I spilled some liquid from my glow stick collection on myself. However I realized my mother threw all my glow sticks away after watching a day time talk show special on how raves were Satan's gateway into an impressionable teenager's life. Before the word "crap" could even leave my lips both my hands erupting in a light more blinding than looking directly into those moving spotlights they set up for premieres and store openings.

I'd like to imagine I didn't have the most awkward First Awake in existence. I'd like to believe I placed beyond the top 50 and saved myself from those unfortunate enough to realize their "gifts" in the bathroom or mid make out session with their significant other. But tripping all over your room in your monkey boxers, accidently turning on loud white girl Rock and blinding yourself kind of takes the cake.

Eventually I turned off the lights and packed my stuff for the open road, a new life waiting on me. A mission to either come to grips with my fascinating ability to be a human firefly (as if) or rid myself of these abilities altogether. That's why I was currently holed up inside this warehouse about three miles from my house (I never said I had super speed, okay, and you try finding a bus at 8:50 P.M. on a Sunday).

I heard of some people being able to shut off their powers in a brief window of discovery after the first glimpse of their Meta genes appearance. They did it by focusing hard, concentrating, and shutting it down for good. For some bizarre reason and try as I might I couldn't. Heck, I even tied a spare shirt around my head pretending to be a swami while closing my eyes and humming. No dice. It looked like dealing with my new life as a genetic freak would be a top priority.

I didn't want to adapt and hone my powers. I didn't want to register and join the Grey Academy for Blooming Meta Humans. They seemed too frilly and constantly touted their poster children, Stars and Stripes, on every news story and website. Stars and Stripes were General Liberty's latest young wards and sidekicks (shudder). They followed him wherever he went and had lame catchphrases that sounded ripped from the very plastic action figures adorned in their image. Liberty was alright though, one of the few supes' I actually respect and don't think ill of. But you can't justify a league of lameness with one good seed.

For the last thirty minutes I was casually eating beans and snapping my fingers making light appear from them like a switch.

Man, I wish I could have gotten a cooler Meta gene. Something awesome like telekinesis or teleporting. Nooo, I get stuck with being a freaking night light.

What could I even say if I appeared to thwart some dastardly villain as he attempted to rob a bank?

"Feel free to run evil doer, but you cannot hide from…the light!"

Only when I switched on my awe inspiring powers they couldn't be seen since villains don't seem to rob many banks at night.

"Oh…um, wow, this is awkward. Can you just, um, come over here and cup your hands to my chest?"

My life was over.

★

I scrolled through Browser, the internet's front page of all things current and interesting, on my smart phone. More memes, more cats, nothing unusual or uncommon. One post caught my eye though.

Ask Me Anything: I'm Night Terror, newest signee into the Hall of Champions

Night Terror was a teleporter with possibly the biggest current reputation and media attention. Ever since he stopped that one terrorist group from bombing the Eiffel Tower in France the guy was a hero even among heroes. He could rip open these dark portals, step though them, and open another anywhere relatively close to his position. The portals or rips could be as big as 747's and he could phase objects just as large through them without breaking a sweat.

He just joined America's group of super powered, government sanctioned crime fighters which made headlines ten time zones over. He was a nice guy, 28-years-old, African American, well built. His costume entailed black elbow long gloves and matching knee high tights that became purple upon reaching the torso. His face was partially covered with a black mask only covering his eyes which got tons of buzz since he wasn't afraid of facial recognition software.

For his proof on the AMA he posted a picture in the link of him and his entire baldheaded splendor holding up a handwritten sign saying, "*Howdy Browser!*"

I scrolled down to look at some of the question, not expecting them to be anything besides "ZOMG WEN DID U FIRS KNO U WULD B GRATE?!11?" or "What's your position on the rapid inflation of economic crippling caused by the direct correlation of siphoned Meta gene users and their lobbyist proponents?"

Boring stuff.

One question caught my eye though and it read, "Do you believe every individual can achieve greatness in their lifetime?"

Night Terror posted his reply in the comment section reading, "I grew up in South Detroit to a poor family. My mother was a waitress working the graveyard shift and my dad worked at an insurance company franchise. We didn't have much but we made it work and my parents were the best around. One day while walking with my mother I saw Spades, one of the Hall's founders, fly right over my head leaving a cloud streak close above the buildings. I asked my mom, 'Will I ever be a great hero like Spades?' to which she looked down at me and said, 'Son, you can be a hero without powers and can be even greater. All you have to do, no matter how dark times get, is to believe in yourself and protect those that can't protect themselves'. I've used that philosophy at all times in life and it even came in handy during that fiasco in Paris. So I'll say this to all of you out there, powers or not, just believe in your ability and watch over those around you. I'm sure you'll achieve greatness one day with that in mind."

Believe in myself and protect others, huh?
I tossed my red rubber ball in the air and caught it again and again, thinking about what he said.
Its supe' mumbo-jumbo but stands to reason. Maybe I should just quit screwing around and register...
I shook my head, clarity taking over its rightful place in my head once more. There was *no* freaking way I was going to strap on tights and gallivant around rooftops. Besides, even if I did I couldn't compete with my lame "super" ability to go luminescent at a moment's notice. Most I could do is operate as a living, breathing lighthouse and the human resources people would be all over that. So my fate was clear and outlined: I had no choice but to run away from this horrible curse. And my intention was to run away until my legs couldn't run anymore.

The next morning I woke up groggily and unceremoniously. It was 10 o'clock according to my phone, Amish time as far as most teenagers were concerned. I got up, stretching my lanky body to shake away some of the morning paralysis. I posed in front of a nearby broken mirror checking myself out. I almost thought I looked good in my faded Hamilton & Saxon T-shirt and baggy jeans. Almost.

I remembered. I hadn't showered or shaved in over a day and the smell was in front of me more than my 17-year-old, light skinned body.

My mother always said, "Honey, I was already light when your father met me. You're well on your way to be the reddest red-bone in the country."

I chuckled, remembering that day fondly when both mom and dad discussed my heritage. Mom's side of the family is Creole, taking roots from New Orleans. Dad's more British than a grey sky raining tea in England. They met while in college, married, yadda yadda yadda, and perfect family stuff. They settled down in California in the small town of Pattisville. Had me, nice life, fast forward 17 years and now I'm on the lamb running with myself *from* myself. My old "Supes' are pukes" shirt in the closet was probably laughing its cotton out.

By now they'd be looking for me but I didn't intend for them to find me. The goal was to work my way up to Washington and reformat my identity. I graduated high school early with excellent grades so I could make do with a minimum wage salary and one bedroom apartment. I'd even call old mum and dad on an untraceable line and tell them I was alright. An excuse would be mandatory. Right now I was torn between being placed in the witness protection program after seeing a mob shooting and my falling in love with a girl who suddenly decided we should elope.

One was unfortunately more believable than the other.

Before making my way to the bus stop I experimented a little with my new ill-gotten pains. I could project light a little further now. Not only that but I could throw little balls of light that seemed to have light substance. They'd hit some of the target cans I placed around the warehouse and, before dissipating, lightly move them, not making them fall down however.

Oh yeah, the amazing Light Bright. Can offer as a substitute glow stick with free light tickle! Greaaaat.

The bus was on time (a first) and I hopped on quickly, hood on my tan jacket up and head down. Pattisville was a small town and I didn't want someone yelling at the top of their lungs, "Lord, it's that Glen

Matterson boy! Someone call up the local police, he's been found!"

No holes precipitation on my parade day, thanks.

Luckily no one noticed and I got off near the St. Roseburg train station. I popped open a vending machine pastry and can of soda before easing onto one of the green benches near the platform. So far so good, the train was going to arrive in about 10 minutes and would take me roughly 90 minutes north where I could either continue my journey by metro train which would bank me all the way to Washington or make use of the local airport, either was viable but one had a bigger risk of getting caught. I'd deal with that problem when I got to it.

While enjoying my nice little perch with my head held back I suddenly felt a kick to my ankles followed by the sound of shuffled clothing. I snapped out of my Zen-like state and saw a flash of black falling to the ground. I just tripped someone by accident and quickly got up to make sure they were okay.

"Crap, sorry...dude? Dude? Dude. I wasn't looking where my feet were," I stammered, my hands hovering over the person I almost helped perform an Olympic dive onto the cement.

The guy smacked my hands away, gruffly cursing under his breath. He stood up, pulled back his slick, white hair and turned my way. He was about my age, little bit shorter and looked... smug. Either he picked his outfit by choice or his dresser had a seizure because he was donned in a black cape with black and green royal attire. He looked more like a young duke than a Roseburgian waiting for the 3:05. Before he even opened his mouth I already had a spot on guess as to what his voice would sound like.

"Watch where your commoner feet are you cur. Stupid Americans are all the same," he spat with a foreign, European accent.

Ever meet someone whom you just wanted to punch regardless of knowing their personal history or back story? Well these hands did more than attract moths but I let go of my balled fists.

"Sorry, man. Really wasn't looking out, my bad."

The white haired kid flicked his cape and turned on a dime, not giving me the slightest hint of acknowledgment as he paraded down the platform. I could practically see the rose petals falling in his presence.

What a freak. But I guess he's more normal than me at the moment. I'd rather be a normal royal jerk with a pole stuck up my butt than a mutated freak any day.

Mr. Black and Far From Mild was gone past the far off pillars and, as far as I was concerned, out of memory. I resumed my previously relaxed position, running my fingers through my short curly hair. I'd seen weirder people and who knows; maybe he was just cosplaying some character from an anime or video game. Cons were popular down here. Before I could even finish my pastry the train loudly blared and pulled slowly along the rails.

Washington, ho.

The train ride was comfy. I had the cart practically to myself as it was a slow day and leaned onto my knapsack with a sigh. Soon I was nodding off to sleep, the bumping train rocking me to sleep like a baby in a crib...

"And now presenting the latest member into the Hall of Champions: Glen Matterson! Let's give him a round of applause everyone!"

The sound of clapping and cheers was deafening in the stadium. Even louder than a jet engine fused with a cranky two-year-old. All around me, literally, all around me were people dressed in formal attire. It was like the football stadium had a gala and half the population of the country decided to make it.

I noticed some people sitting in a row either side of the podium where the announcer had just said my name. In the red, cushioned seats were-

Oh god, no.

"It can't be," I muttered, barely hearing myself over the pandemonium.

In that row were the world's best and most accomplished superheroes. Talon, Binary Helios, Miss Destruction, if they had saved the world at least once they were sitting here. And I had a clue why they were sitting here.

I felt a pair of hands push me, snapping me out of my dazed state. I almost fell over on the large red velvet rug that was underneath the podium containing the microphone which only amplified my ungraceful display.

"I-um, wow, h-hi there everyone," I slowly muttered out, my mind blank but knowing full well of what I was here for. I didn't want to admit it and I had a ray of hope that if I didn't it would all just go away. However, before I could lull myself into my wonderful false sense of security the announcer seized the mic.

"Ain't he cute boys and gals? Well we all know why we're here and that is this: to welcome young Glen into the upper echelons of the Hall, also known as the Presidium!"

I choked on my spit.

It was worse than I thought. I was bypassing the entry level league and was joining the cream of the crop and humanity's first line of defense: The Presidium, a handful of heroes that weren't just the best in the world but the galaxy.

Crapcrapcrapcrapcrapcrapcrap.

"Glen will join the best of the best on Sanctuary and will serve as a personal sidekick to…well…EVERYONE!" He exclaimed making the stadium erupt in a roar.

I fainted on the spot.

I awoke with a start accompanied by a sharp pain in my head. I smacked the low support bar head on after escaping my nightmare. Some people have bad dreams about ax murdering psychopaths; some experience a recurring loop of falling but never reaching the ground. Me? I had nightmares about joining masked weirdos in their holy fight for justice.

Shudder.

While rubbing my head with my free hand I checked my phone. Just 30 minutes to go until the next checkpoint. More distance away from whatever fate awaited me if I stayed in Pattisville. Mom would probably discover my "talents" and attempt to throw a big party, dad would rain on her parade by mentioning I must maintain a secret identity, they'd call the National Meta Human Crisis hotline and sooner or later I'd be shipped to the academy where I'd spend my free time sleeping and breathing *Villain Psychology* or *Spandex or Tights: Costuming 101.*

I'd rather choke on a rat.

But despite opting for a rodent firmly lodged in my windpipe I pondered that life. How maybe I'd make some new friends, make myself a better (partly) human being, do some good in the world. Maybe this wasn't the end of my life but the beginning. I flicked my fingers which shot out a prism of light, pushing one of my clothes to the still shaking floor. My powers were changing, growing, fulfilling the exact law of Meta gene biology: the first 72 hours after first awakening the abilities only accelerate rapidly until reaching full immersion in the DNA and settling at a base form.

Well I was approximately 27 in and if I could knock stuff over with actual mass generated from me and who knows what else I could do. It vexed me inside, stirring up my insides; some considered this a once in a lifetime chance, gaining something supernatural in a world where power was how far you could exceed human restraints. Some spent their entire life dedicated to finding their own Meta gene only to end up in a well of depression or loathing.

Why me?

My wonderful angst-y state didn't last long because boom. No, you misunderstand me, *boom.* Explosion, bang, whatever your preference or choice of what to call it had just taken place, sending my eardrums caving in and forcing me into a fetal position.

The world was spinning and I was in the air, a slave to ragdoll physics which made me slam ribs first into the hard plastic seats. The air swam out of my lungs and my brain went fuzzy on impact. I just stayed exactly like that, gasping for air like a beached whale, half of my body on the seat and the other half hanging out into the aisle. It took several minutes to regain my composure until I was ready, despite nearly falling, to stand to my feet. Blood was in my mouth, the thick taste of iron dripping down my throat. I shook my head and swallowed. It was only from biting the inside of my lip from the…from the…

Just what freakin' was that?

I opened the doors between the carts and swiftly climbed the attached ladder. Whatever had happened wasn't colossally bad or a bleeding lip would be the least of my problems. The train had stopped but I didn't sense any major danger. Either way you slice it I had to get up on the train and see what had just rocked my world, literally.

I jumped up onto the metal with a light tap and began to survey the wreck. All the carts were intact and had small dents, scratches, nothing big. The lead cart…that was a different story. It was smoking with no flames emerging from the windows but was on its side, a wounded steel titan. That wasn't the sight that caught my attention, though. It was *who* that was on top that got my attention.

Lo and behold Mr. Dark and Edgy, Sir Prude Buttface IV in the flesh.

Buttface was grasping the conductor by the neck that, in turn, was moving his dangling feet in a poor attempt to touch solid ground. Anger flowed through me, partly because of the sight of Punksworth hoisting a poor innocent guy by his neck, partly because I just knew whatever in the hell had just happened he was the cause. My rage frothed over and made its way into my vocal chords.

"Hey! Loser in the black and green! Let the guy go!" I boomed, somehow able to make my voice heard over the sound of the now stationary creaking locomotive.

He turned my way slowly, inch by inch, like had all the time in the world to address what rude outburst had directed itself his way. He was still grasping the poor conductor by the neck, a squirming mess of blue uniform. Upon finally seeing the person from which the demand came from he let the man down, far from gently, the conductor stumbling away.

"Well, well, if it isn't Mr. Stupid American!" He scoffed, superiority and foreignness mixed into his tone, "Why, Mr. Stupid American, do you like my work?"

He beckoned around him, showcasing the derailed train which dazed passengers were streaming out.

"You prick, didn't your mother tell you trains were meant to stay on the tracks? Just what did you do?"

He laughed, a booming, annoying, snarky, conceited (okay, if it wasn't clear so far I did not like the guy) display of amusement.

"Simple. I merely forced us to make a stop. Now as to the instrument of said stopping it was this," he held up his hand, sparking with crackling electricity, "and this," his other hand held up a small octagonal device emblazoned with a fancy S on it. That S...that logo...it was the same design as-

No way.

"Just where in god's name did you get Strauss-Tech merchandise?" I inquired in disbelief.

He chuckled, walking over to me with loud clunks as his boots hit the metal.

"Perhaps because I am in fact, a Straussburg?"

Electricity shot from his hands with a crack sending him into the air like a cannon. He propelled himself in my direction stopping short of my position by about three meters.

Oh freaking great. I have a member of the royal family of Straussland up in my grill right now and of course he can shoot bloody thunder from his fingertips. Peachy.

"You'll have to pardon my Strauss brand enhancer pendants," he held up his hands which had small, black half spheres on them, "My Meta gene only just appeared roughly two days ago and these concentrate the power."

Are you serious? Was this a poorly written drama or was I just wildly unlucky?

He motioned forward causing me to edge back. He noticed and smugly chuckled.

"On the cautious side, I see? Well, with due reason. You don't even have any powers, wretch. But despite being a weakling I might as well introduce the bringer of your death. Viktor von Straussburg, heir to the Straussburg family and future ruler of Straussland, jewel of Europe and harbinger of the world. I wish I could say I am pleased to make your acquaintance but alas, I am not."

With one hand outstretched in my direction like a cannon readying

for fire he began charging his electricity into the half orb.

This was bad, majorly, majorly bad. I had a prince of a country possibly bearing WMD's about to fry me extra crispy and what could I do to defend myself? Perform a light show sans the 80's Power Ballad Rock music? I was screwed.

This was it. This was really the end. Because of my inability to come to grips with myself I was now going to pass on to the next life in a spark of non-glory. The wilderness around me, brimming with yellowing trees and tall grass would be my final resting place. I wouldn't even have enough to fill a casket as I was sure whatever power Viktor had would singe and scatter my atoms. I'd be nothing but a smudge and a memory.

Sorry mom, dad. I guess you really will believe I'm dead. I didn't even get to hear your voices one last time...

I swallowed, closed my eyes, and awaited my fate.

But instead of the sound of one Glen Matterson becoming said smudge, a voice above me took its place.

Loud.

Commanding.

Filled with...bravado.

"Stop *right* there, Viktor von Straussburg or you'll have to face me: the champion of the downtrodden!"

Crap.

"Hero of justice!"

No please no, I'll take electrocution.

"The one and only: General Liberty!"

I opened my eyes if only to confirm what fate worse than molecule scattering lay before me. There, hovering above us in mid-air was Uncle Sam's finest, old Liberty himself.

He looked exactly like he was displayed in the pictures: bulging muscles practically tearing from his red and blue costume, a minimally designed eagle forming the crest on his chest, and white lined mask adorning his head. The possibly most loved hero in the world and almost the most flamboyant, was right here on the 3:05 line. Even worse: he had just *saved* me.

I felt dirty.

"Well if it isn't the blue steel himself. I was wondering when the Hall would attempt to stop me but oh, never did I think I'd get America's finest!"

"Shut it, Viktor, I know just exactly what you're here for," the General boomed, his voice vibrating the train. Stupid supersonic voice projection.

He continued, "We were monitoring you the moment you blew your nose on U.S. soil. What I can't figure out is why you decided to make a scene so far away from the nuclear plant."

What. Nuclear plant? Just what is going on here? Am I in the middle of another stupid supe' and baddy stand off?

Viktor just stayed calm and collected, gathering himself before finally speaking.

"So the people can know, Liberty."

"Know what?" His voice inquired, shaking the train once more.

"So they'll know that no matter which hero they tossed at me it would be pointless. No one can stop me and as the mushroom cloud rises high into the sky with the stained blood of millions the people will cry out, 'Why didn't our heroes save us?' only for the crude realization to hit: they couldn't. No hero could or can save them from the events of life and goodness in the world has perished.

Christ, he was going to start an actual war between Straussland and the U.S. with the lives of innocent people as the pretext. I was looking at a teenage Gavrilo Principe.

The general just laughed though, unfazed by whatever threats or plots Viktor had going around in his conceited head.

"And, pray tell, how do you intend to do that when you're around... oh...2000 miles away from Nevada?"

Viktor responded with his own laugh. Hero-villain 101: both laughed a lot.

"With...this!" He held up what appeared to be a slim but fairly big black screen from his back.

He brandished it towards the floating crusader, energy suddenly awakening it into a complex looking, expanded mechanical form. It looked like an old computer.

"Ooh, what's that going to do, read a floppy disk," I said, my first time speaking while General Liberty arrived.

"SILENCE, WELP!" Viktor spat, eyes blazing and nostrils flaring at me.

Apparently this was a big moment for him and I was ruining it with my quips. Poor kid, not every baddy gets to exchange banter with a Hall member shortly after getting his Meta gene. This was a one in a million party and I just crashed it by being number two. Viktor regained his composure and continued.

"This is a developmental warp device. All I have to do is flick this switch and I'll be teleported to the Isotech nuclear plant. Even with your top speed you won't get there in time, Liberty. And if you put the call in no one's even around Nevada to begin with."

So that was the game. Rubbing it in the head superhero's face before slaughtering millions with potential billions as the world was plunged into war once more. Don't teenagers just read books anymore?

Liberty veered down but Viktor was too fast. Within milliseconds he activated the teleport device and it shined almost as brightly as me. Something was wrong though since he was in his exact same position.

"Blast it, bloody thing...mu-," he got cut off.

His body surged in my direction with a mechanical whir emitted from his machine. I didn't have time to get out of the way as he collided with me, full force, making me lose consciousness. My world went black for the second time today.

Everything hurt.

I was going to puke. My *body* felt like it was going to puke. It was like someone stuck me inside a giant blender and had poured me back into the world. I didn't want to puke but my stomach vetoed that idea.

I stood up, eyes still closed, wiping the undigested Happy Cappy pastry remains from my chin, trying to remember what had happened before I went black.

Viktor derailed a train, check.

Liberty showed up, check.

Viktor teleported leaving for the power plant, check.

I was still on said derailed train...unchecked.

I opened my eyes and took in the image around me. I was on flat, arid ground with a stretching chain link fence bordering the new area. Sporadic clumps of dead grass popped up breaking the pattern of sandy dirt and I was pretty sure I heard a coyote's howl in the distance. This meant I was... oh boy.

I turned around to meet a two hundred foot nuclear silo towering above me like a monument to god. Viktor's device had worked. We were at the Isotech plant which meant doomsday was going to happen; only I was just a little closer to the event horizon than everyone else.

Nuts.

"Ugh... stupid interns... never entrust spatial and time based technology to a bunch of rookies."

Viktor's voice came from the side of the silo, his limping body easing around it and coming into focus. So it had worked... but... I noticed something. It was darker. Like dusk. Nevada was in the same time zone as Cali so why was the sun creeping down the horizon?

"Hey, Prince Angstmaster."

Good one, Glen.

"Why is it darker? We teleported right? And if we were really unconscious for like four hours wouldn't Liberty be here by now?"

Viktor stopped.

"Hm hm hm, yes but see that's just the thing. This device also transports one not just through space but *time*. That setting, I thought, hadn't been programmed for this mission but interns are just oh so idiotic and infantile."

Made sense and explained the waning day time. But what I wasn't clear on was why half the Hall wasn't here waiting for him. Unless...

"Looks like they thought we perished!" Viktor excitedly shook. "The energy signature must have read we never reappeared and even if they did inspect this area they wouldn't find anything! They'd move on and continue saving cats in trees. There's no one here to stop me!"

This is bad; this is really, monumentally, colossally, gargantuan bad. This lunatic's going to blow up the western sea board and there's no one with any power to sto-.

I froze.

Oh no. No, no, no, no, HECK to the no.

There was someone here to stop him, someone with a very intact Meta gene and he was standing in the middle of the dessert in high tops and blue jeans. Me.

"You're not getting away with this," I weakly said aloud.

"Oh... what are you going to do Normy? Trip on me? I could fry you like a fish and move on to that control room," he motioned toward the adjacent building, "before you even stopped breathing."

It was true. I possibly wouldn't be able to stop him and would only lose my life quicker. But I had to try. Even if I didn't want to assume the role of hero there was no one else to take the mantle.

"The only way you'll be getting to that control room is over my cold, dead, mulatto carcass!" I yelled, adrenaline running through my veins.

"That... can be arranged," he lowly responded.

Viktor charged his hands with blue, crackling electricity and brought his arms in front of him. With a loud snap the power surged forth, right in my direction.

As a gut reflex I closed my eyes, brought my arms in front of me to protect from what was possibly millions of volts and prepared for the pain.

Pain that hadn't come yet. Or now. Or now. Or even now. Sheesh, wasn't lightning supposed to be quick?

I opened my eyes to discover just why I wasn't an original recipe Glen right now. I was in a bubble of transparent light, completely surrounding me above and below. I brought my hand out to touch it and upon feeling the thick plastic-like matter it hummed.

Did I...do this?

But I could feel like I did. This was from me. This was my energy and it had just saved me from Viktor's spark of death. A rush overcame me. I could defend myself from this nut-job and possibly stop him before he could even activate the other silos adjourning the nuclear site. Viktor looked stunned.

"OH COME ON! My very first time going through with a plot and I get stopped by a male fairy!" He rambled, moving on to curse in a language I didn't understand.

"Well if you like that then I have more tricks, pretty boy," I growled, snapping my fingers and bringing the barrier down.

I mimicked the same technique as Viktor and shot light from my hands. I concentrated harder than on the train and could feel myself generating heat and mass from my hands. It was different, harder, and rougher. This could actually do some damage. I released the energy which shot out, a glowing tank engine barreling its way towards Viktor. My attack hit him directly and he went flying into the air like a ballerina.

Cool.

I watched him with baited breath. It wasn't enough to kill him, I knew my own new strength, just stop him. He groaned making me release my held breath.

"Stupid...bloody...American...supes'. I *(hack)* can't believe *(wheeze)* you have the gall *(cough)* to strike me, the future king," he whispered in his crumpled state.

That wasn't enough though as soon he was back on his feet and looking meaner than ever. His eyes went completely blue and I could feel static in the air. He was emitting sparks in every direction as his fury translated into electrical energy. A walking electric plant was marching to me *inside* a nuclear plant. If I had to arrange a list of places not to be in this would take the cake.

He lifted his hands to the sky and I immediately felt the atmosphere become heavier. This was bad. He was charging a much stronger attack as was made evident from the lightning striking the ground around him. I exhaled, finally realizing just how tired I was from that one burst of solid light. One more shot was in me but just that one. If only he was closer, I could just use a point blank blast on him possibly brining him down. If only he were closer...if only he-.

An idea smacked me across the face like an imaginary hand.

Monologue.

If there was one thing villains, even junior ones like him, liked doing it was monologuing. Right before victory could be grasped they just *had* to reveal their intentions, how clever they were for triumphing over the opposition, the universe spread out just for their claiming. They all did it and Viktor, hopefully, wouldn't be an exception. It was worth a shot.

I threw my hands in the air and went to my knees.

"I give up."

Viktor looked down and froze mid charge. Incredulousness was present on his face.

"What?" He said in disbelief.

"I give up, there's no way I could beat someone as... as *powerful* as you" I groaned, defeat dripping in my tone.

The energy dissipated and Viktor went to his normal pretentious but not sparking form. Part one was complete.

"I-I mean, just *look* at you! You're possibly the most powerful super villain on the planet! Way stronger than Warbeast or Revengeant."

Viktor looked like he got a smug Botox injection.

"But... just tell me this, before you send me into the next world... how did you come up with this evil plan?"

The bait was set and all he had to do was nibble the cheese. No baddy on the planet could miss such an opportunity like this especially someone on their first wicked scheme.

"Oh... well... this is sudden," he paused, not knowing where to start first, "Well...hm... I got the idea while in the spa one day getting a Double Cucumber Divinity Relaxer."

Prick.

"I just didn't know what to do with myself when I had the bright idea of making daddy proud and blowing a quarter of the U.S. to kingdom come!" He frantically continued, "Then imagine my surprise when my long awaited meta gene present in my family's royal, holy, famed bloodline appeared! I decided to make my way to America, use the teleport device and not only attack people's physical but *emotional* forms when their precious heroes were powerless to stop them!"

Craze was splashing from his mouth, his tirade long and self-righteous.

Perfect.

He loomed closer and closer to me, a warrior walking to claim his defeated opponent.

"And now," he stopped, standing just inches away from me, his form above mine, "I will send you into the next world with the force containing millions of volts of electricity. My first hero killed and first ploy successful. The world shall be mine soon enough and it starts with you. Now, await my judgment."

His hand rose to the sky.

Gotcha.

"Sweet dreams pretty boy," I uttered.

It all happened very quickly. I charged all of my remaining energy into my hands, stabilized it and exploded it outward, a brilliance of light. Viktor went sailing towards the silo, his body hitting it with an anticlimactic thud. Sparkles took his former place and his path into the titanium behemoth. It was like Viktor could fly and his pixie dust traced his wake. He fell to the ground from the non-lethal height of several meters and remained stationary. No getting up, no further world ruining tactics. Just him taking a nap like a little baby.

Whew.

I had done it. I'd stopped a madman from destroying the west coast and plunging the world into another war. I was a... hero.

Son of a-

My body gave out and weakness claimed my limbs. That last surge of power had sapped me of my remaining strength and I didn't even possess the ability to stand. But it didn't matter. I was happy. Who cared if I was the very thing I had detested my whole life. It felt good. I saved people. Maybe this whole hero business wasn't all that bad.

I faded into unconscious but not without a grin on my face.

★

"And you're sure about this? I mean, you don't have to join the academy, you could just go back to your, well, partly normal life."

General Liberty had his hand on my shoulder and looked towards the mob of young people clamoring in front of the registration table.

"Yeah, I'm sure. There's no going back to the way things were. Video games, awkward school dances, TV re-runs. Why do that kind of stuff when the good old Grey Academy awaits, you know?" I chimed back.

We were back in California and it was about a week and a half from the Straussburg incident. I had stopped Viktor single-handedly from exploding the Isotech nuclear plant and just teleporting away. Old Vik was now detained in a major juvenile justice complex just for others like him. There was a low chance of any spa treatment there.

I was a hero even though I at first wanted nothing of the sort. Liberty and I were now at the registration table for the Grey Academy which I decided to join. The General suggested I attend and even produced a handwritten letter of recommendation. My acceptance was as good as confirmed. I could practically waltz in with the letter alone without even dropping the "I saved the west coast" line.

Everyone hoping to apply had on a generic Grey Academy mask to spare the identity leaking, myself included. It was a sea of black masked super kids clamoring to be signed up into the highest acclaimed Meta gene school in the country. Like freshman year's club sign ups all over again.

"Well, if you've made up your mind then good on you," Liberty gave my shoulder a pat, his red glove rocking my body with only a tap, "Are you sure you're going to like it there?"

I glanced back to the frenzy when a figure strode past me in slow motion. A gorgeous Asian girl donned in Harajuku attire glided to my side, her detailed and intricately designed boots sounding off and leaving dark, swirling footprints in the pavement with each step. Her black tutu skirt attached to a loosely hanging corset fluttered in the breeze, moving with her like a living organism. She lifted her ponytail up and attached her own mask in one fluid motion, unafraid of revealing her identity. The girl strode into an opening and joined the others applying for the academy.

"Oh yeah, I'm sure" I blubbered back, sappiness in my voice.

I started making my way towards the table and my new future. I didn't know what would happen after joining the school and honing my powers. I didn't know what challenges waited for me or the obstacles sure to be placed in my path but that didn't matter. I would believe in myself and protect others the entire way, Night Terror's own mantra becoming my own. I was a hero and finally accepted that fact with firm resolve. This marked a new chapter in my life.

"Oh, kid, before you go, just in case I need to know who to spread some good words about in the Hall for when you graduate, what's your new name?" Liberty shouted over the bustle of the crowd.

I stopped, turned around, and replied back to him with a wide smile.

"Arclight."

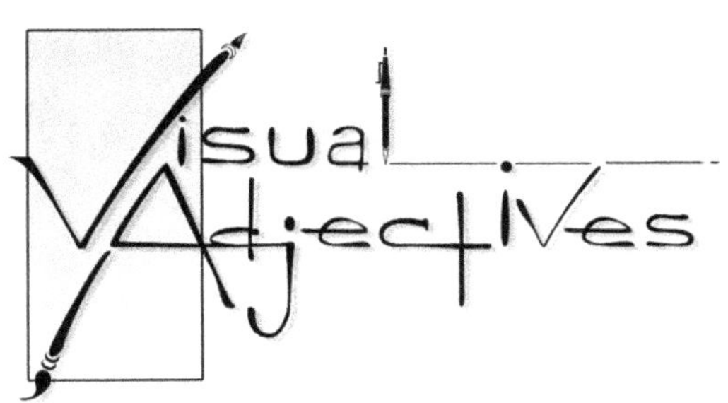